bad Beat

L.M. BENNETT

This one is for all the Phils of poker.
And as always, thank you to my love; my future wife. Thank you for
being you.

Follow L.M. on Threads

Follow L.M. on Instagram

CONTENTS

1. Bluffing for Beginners   1
   2017: Miri

2. Suds   5
   2023: Jax

3. Of Tits and Hissy Fits   9
   Miri

4. Not You Again   15
   Jax

5. Shuffle Up And Deal   21
   Miri

6. Heads Up   27
   Jax

7. Babygirl   33
   Miri

8. Do It In My Name   37
   Jax

9. Bitter Notes   45
    Miri

10. Canary Yellow   49
    Jax

11. Ripples Aren't Just Chips   55
    Miri

12. Advanced Hornet's Nest Kicking Techniques   61
    Jax

13. River Flush or Bust   65
    Miri

14. On The House   69
    Jax

15. King of Spades   79
    Miri

16. Apple Fritters and Regret   83
    Jax

17. If You Can't Spot the Fish...   89
    Jax

18. Philosophy for Wrestlers   99
    Miri

19. The Turn   103
    Jax

20. Suited Connectors   113
    Miri

21. On The Flop   119
    Jax

22. All In   125
    Miri

23. Sucker Free Sunday   131
    Jax

24. On Tilt   139
    Miri

25. Nice to Beat You   147
    Jax

26. Thank You!   153

27. PREVIEW: Tap Out   155

BLUFFING FOR BEGINNERS

2017: MIRI

I magine the Ocean Pearl Poker Room as a movie set under crystal chandeliers, where the tables could've been swiped from a mafioso den. Everyone's face frozen in thought, careful not to give anything away.

In Atlantic City, it was always a crap shoot; the guy next to you could be a gangster, or he could be a used car salesman. Just between us, they dressed the same. Faux-expensive, ill-fitting suits from the back of somebody's dusty closet. At the tables, there were more poker faces here than a Lady Gaga video.

Mama hated gambling. She said, you bet either your dreams or your dignity, and the house usually took one. One bad bet, and you were downstairs with the people in the bus lanes, watching old ladies play Mah Jongg while waiting for a bus back to Manhattan.

Ask me how I know.

I had found myself in this tantalizing, perilous playground, eyes darting among my fellow performers. It was like a casting call for a movie where everyone was vying for the lead role, but no one had gotten the script. And all the good roles were in Las Vegas.

The person sitting at the end of the felt took off dark thick sunglasses to clean them with the hem of their gray hoodie. A chiseled jaw said this was a man, but the brown fingers cleaning the glasses were too delicate to belong to any man. Neat, clean fingernails. Muscled veins and tattoos twitched as they rubbed at the lenses roughly. Call me intrigued.

I continued looking up, but the hoodie was too loose to show whether breasts were underneath. After a moment, those fingers paused cleaning the glasses. Her hard, hooded eyes and thick brows were unnerving. Upon me noticing her, those hooded amber eyes softened with amusement.

I didn't know if this woman was trying to size me up, or take me to bed. Maybe both?

"I don't normally get this kind of attention. Should I be worried?"

"No. But now you can add 'being stared at' to the list of talents you possess." Better to shut that *all* the way down. I was here to win.

The woman recoiled as if stung. "And you can add 'being rude' to yours?"

Piotr Mazur took the unlit cigar from his lips, revealing nicotine-stained teeth. He tapped the felt table with it. I frowned. "I suggest we—let us change the topic, yes?" Piotr waved his arms around, looking like the table's elder statesman, just like he always did on tv. Except shorter. Everyone looked taller on television. "Poker is about the skill, not the drama. Let us play."

"Indeed." I nodded. Now that I had won enough to keep the bill collectors happy, there was a pair of tall red-bottom heels in one of the outlet stores downstairs with my name on them.

If I played this hand right, maybe I could even get a purse to match.

After the blinds put up their bets, the dealer shuffled the cards, burning the top card.

I could still feel the same pair of hooded eyes on me, but I ignored them to pretend to look at my hole cards instead.

What did she have?

I had enough of a cushion to lose a few chips to gain some information, and it wasn't even as big a risk as it should be.

Everyone probably thought I was a bimbo, anyway. Prettiest thing in the room, I overheard someone say when I sat down at the table.

The players in between us did a peek and shriek and tossed their cards back to the green felt. She stayed in.

What if I played the person instead of the cards, just this once? What would happen?

I paused a moment to lift up my cards again, then looked at the shadow of felt under my fingers. One of the cards was a face card. King? Queen? Who cared.

I plopped the cards back down on the table, and picked up a small stack of chips. Three hundred should be enough to see if this worked. My red bottoms were waiting.

I took a deep breath and pushed the chips forward. This wasn't a bluff, I was looking for information. I wanted to see how strong Hooded Eyes hand was; or at least, how much she thought it was worth. The urge to look across the felt tugged at me more, and it annoyed me. I gave in.

Surprise, Hooded Eyes was looking at me right back. Caught, the woman fiddled with her chips. The glasses lay discarded on the table next to her. She spoke.

"That's a big bet. What do you think I'm holding?" She studied me openly, separating the stack of chips and then sliding them back together again, like a deck of cards.

I met her gaze and raised an eyebrow.

"Oh, I think you're holding something worth betting on," I said, fluttering my eyelashes. The good mink ones that made your eyes look doe soft. Especially when you were running over people at the table. "The question is, how much is it worth it to you to find out what I have?"

Hooded Eyes leaned back. Trying to project strength, probably something she read from some antiquated 1980s poker manual. But, the interesting thing was, the rigid tilt of her body spoke volumes. Her back was stiff as a board. She cleared her throat, frowning. I refused to even blink first. She kept her face stony and unreadable, her chest rising slowly. Then, dear Lord, Hooded Eyes folded her cards up and tossed them onto the felt.

The dealer pushed a stack of chips over to me, bigger than any stack I'd seen so far.

Holy shit, it worked!

Just to be a stinker, I turned up my cards. Queen-Three.

I glanced up at Hooded Eyes once more, relishing the salty way she sucked her teeth. Piotr raised a glass of brown liquor in my direction, and I finally allowed myself to smile.

SUDS

2023: JAX

I wasn't sure what turned me off first. Airport parking. The thought of winding lines full of bored-looking passengers in never-ending lines, maybe. Walking through the metal detectors. Intrusive pat downs. Watery, overpriced drinks. Fake smiles, polite conversations with people you will never meet again in life. Neck pillows. Hot, late July sun, and long shuttle lines. Rental cars. I couldn't do it. Not today.

My reasonable side said it was probably three hours, tops, from my doorstep to the room waiting for me at Lucky Skies. But this was too important because my mind was full of thoughts and it shouldn't be. They weren't two million dollar thoughts, and that's all I was willing to make time for right now.

No. Instead, I needed me, the open road, and some music. The Los Angeles skyline melted into highways that gave way to gravel, dirt, mountains, and a sunset, scored to Yacht Rock. That's it. It was twenty-four hours before the tournament, and all I wanted was calm and focus.

What Dru wanted was to see if I really meant it when I said, "Be gone when I get back." To her, that meant a string of text messages with the most creative language I had heard since the last time I cut someone off in traffic. We're talking vulgar sex acts and long dead relatives creative, here. When I took my phone off airplane mode to plug in the casino's address, a barrage of messages popped up. Today, she wanted to be sweet. She had gone from threatening me with a visit from her cousins to wanting to see me "just to talk."

The time to talk would've been before she took the liberty of tossing my PlayStation into the dishwasher. Or, before she made confetti out of the 1989 winning tournament card Ms. Enid Torres had signed for me.

She had no regard for money, least of all mine. I flicked off each pop up as it flashed across the top of my screen.

Hey, I was wondering—delete.

When you get to Vegas, Jax, we need to—no. Delete.

I know you're upset, but let's talk about this—I'm done talking. Delete.

The only way I was going to get rid of her—for now anyway—was to go nuclear. Pressing the 'block' button felt like raking in a huge pot after heads-up at the final table. A fat white gold and diamond tournament bracelet heavy on my wrist, and a two million dollar check with my name on it. The tournament director and host standing on either side of me holding a big check with me in the middle, flashing all my teeth.

While I'm disappointed in having to miss the moment she realized her blue text messages were turning green, it was for the best.

I would not allow her to ruin this moment for me. The money well was dry. She loved it more than me. I was done throwing it at her to keep her on my arm and in my bed.

Miles of asphalt stretched out before me as the sun dipped lower in the sky. I hummed along to songs I only half knew and tapped the wheel in time with the beat of nostalgic music. As blue skies turned dusky pink and gold, my car ate gravel like it was starved.

When the signs on the road named exits for Las Vegas, a smile pulled up my face. Openly, proudly, I sang off-key. Anyone who pulled up next to my car would be amused at my solo car karaoke. Hell, maybe it was me who was starving?

If I won this tournament bracelet, would I be like one of those broad-shouldered football dudes on TV whose championship rings winked at the camera whenever they were explaining a play? Probably.

I was getting ahead of myself.

If I didn't take home this bracelet, it wasn't about missing out on the prize money, although that would suck, too. It was about my name, my reputation. This was my shot to prove I wasn't just another online fish in deep water with the sharks, but a real contender. A loss here would echo through the halls of every poker room, branding me a wannabe. But a win would be real sweet. Cake sweet. A chance to hear my name mentioned along with some of the same players I lost sleep studying.

Then there was Dru. Winning the tournament would mean finally breaking free from her, from the toxic spiral I'd found myself in. Nobody wants to start over again, right? You can only tolerate someone's favorite colors and Grand Rising texts until the idea of dating started to feel like a missed gut shot straight, but I couldn't be her sponsor anymore when I wanted to be her lover instead.

It would mean having the freedom to build my life alone. Going for dolo. With no one in my corner, the stakes were higher than they'd ever been. Yet, I was ready to go all in.

Somewhere, right now, other women were driving and flying into Las Vegas, too. Each planning, plotting, forming blueprints, so they'd end up at the final table holding the nut flush to win the same bracelet I wanted. Two hundred of us, I'd heard. Buy-in had been open a whole hour before they had to shut it down.

I've just got to beat all 199 of them to win it for myself.

Easy peasy. Right?

OF TITS AND HISSY FITS

MIRI

The flashing neon lights of the Lucky Skies casino seared my eyes as I stepped out of the town car. Even at night it was still warm, like all that dry heat got trapped in the rocks during the day and it all let out on the Strip at night.

I slid on my sunglasses to cut the glare, ignoring the wolf whistles and leers from the crowd of frat boys lingering by the entrance. Let them stare.

"Right this way, Ms. Black," the bellhop said, holding open the door for me.

I followed him through the glass doors, chin lifted high.

Another video surfaced last night. Some pizza-faced moron with coke-bottle glasses and a dollar-store webcam claimed I flashed my tits and batted my eyelashes to distract players.

I rolled my eyes. Give me more credit than that, *please*. As if I ever stuck out my tits with no kind of strategy at all. Mama taught me way better than that.

The bellhop droned on about the penthouse amenities, a rooftop pool, an executive concierge, VIP access to clubs, and a private chef.

Nothing special.

I was so lost in thought, I almost didn't notice her.

Jax.

Our eyes met for a split second before I looked away from those amber eyes that never, ever gave anything away.

Her swagger, her cool arrogance, the wry tilt of her thick lips. Everything about her annoyed me. It had since we had met years earlier and I made her look stupid trying to call me out for staring at her.

I would do it again. Right at this tournament where I'd claim my next bracelet.

Hopefully, I'd be sitting across from her as she twirled her last lonely chip across the felt to me as the tournament director slipped on my bracelet and handed me a fat two million-dollar check.

"Actually, I'll wait for the next one," I told the bellhop. I didn't want to spend one more second in her presence than I had to.

Jax stepped into the elevator and turned to face front as the doors slid closed. I didn't miss her little smirk as she turned away, but when she looked back, her expression was pure stone. That was her poker face at work.

I knew her tells, though. The way she toyed with her chips when bluffing. How her left eyebrow twitched when she had a good hand. Tiny details revealed the cracks in her stoic mask.

She was a worthy opponent, no doubt. Some even called her the Ice Queen. But underneath a cool facade lay a fiery competitor. I saw it in the ferocity of her bets and the intensity in those dark eyes. She wouldn't hold back today.

Good. I wanted a challenge. Her skills would sharpen my own. When I took her down, my victory would be even sweeter.

Where Jax was ice, I was fire. My poise and subtle tells lured others into underestimating me. Only a fool would dismiss the sharp mind behind my elegant facade.

I'd carved out my place in this world through sheer determination and grit.

For too long, the old boys' club tried to keep me in my place, ignore me, push me aside. Those days were over the year I pushed Piotr out of his tenth bracelet with pocket Queens. The symbolism wasn't lost on me.

Now, when I swept into a room in designer dresses and red bottoms, they saw the next champion. I'd fought hard for my legacy, and no one was taking it from me.

Not some loser taking up space in his mother's basement, and especially not Jax.

The doors slid open, and I stepped into the penthouse suite. Plush carpets, granite counters, floor-to-ceiling windows overlooking the glittering skyline, furniture that cost more than most people's cars—the room oozed luxury. I reveled in it; a testament to my hard-won success.

The bellhop tossed my bag on the suitcase rack next to the California King bed and headed straight for the minibar.

"Compliments of the hotel. Please let us know if you need anything else."

Tempranillo. I touched the cool bottle and poured myself a splash. Perfectly chilled.

I refilled my glass, savoring the wine's cherry and cedar notes. A knock at the door interrupted my reverie.

"Room service," a man called out. The bellhop immediately sprang into action, opening the door to a server wheeling in a cart laden with covered dishes. He transferred them to the dining table with crisp efficiency.

My executive concierge, Tisha, hadn't skipped a single line of my instructions. I'd have to make sure she got a nice tip for her attention to detail.

After he left, I lifted the cloche off the main plate. A filet mignon drizzled with béarnaise sauce, roasted asparagus spears on the side. I took a bite of the perfectly cooked beef, then another sip of wine.

As I ate, my thoughts drifted back to Jax. That woman was a puzzle I needed to solve. On the surface she was cool as ice, emotions sealed up in amber-colored eyes, tucked away tight behind those devastating cheekbones. But I sensed a fire in her waiting to ignite. What would it take to unleash her barely contained passion?

As I sipped, I gazed out at the Vegas skyline glittering below.

From up here, the world felt small and conquerable, like this tournament. I'd need to play tight early on, feeling out the competition before raising the stakes.

Patience was key.

Let them reveal their tells, then exploit every weakness. My pulse quickened as I envisioned the final table, just Jax and me remaining.

Her eyes would narrow when I pushed all my chips to the center. Was I bluffing, or did I have the winning hand? She'd toy with her bracelet, considering her options. Finally, she'd call, unable to resist finding out.

Then I would flip my cards, revealing the flush draw that crushed her two pair. Her stony expression would crack for an instant when she realized I'd bested her. Again.

I smiled, adrenaline already pumping through my veins. Time to remind them why I'm that bitch. Ms. Poker. With skill, nerve and a little luck, that bracelet would soon be mine.

Time to shuffle up.

NOT YOU AGAIN

JAX

There's nothing like a casino in the middle of July.

Safe from the blistering heat of outside, the crowds of sweaty people carrying neon guitars filled with melting liquor slush. Past those doors, the slot machines blend to become a gentle hum that only draws your feet down the stairs into the casino floor, past the smoking section, video poker and penny slots. Whoops, bells and claps accompany the sound of machines promising to hit the bonus diamond level, only to spit out a bonus $2 as Mr. Big feeds Carrie some lie she's always wanted to hear about herself. To my left, Bones insisted he's a doctor, not a mechanic as a wheel spun faster, red, yellow, blue blurred to warp speed, as a white-haired woman looked up. For her trouble, she won $11.47. Much less than the 15x the prize she had hoped to win, it's a sneeze lost at the last second. Undeterred, she slapped the flashing button again immediately.

That's how they trapped you.

I tried to leave Las Vegas. Packed my bags and moved to L.A. But that doesn't really work when two weeks of work earns a year's salary.

A waitress balancing a tray of drinks almost clashed with me, expertly swerving out of the way at the last moment. She brought the older lady something that smelled like a Jack and coke. Turning to her, I saw the woman's profile and grinned. Out of all the faces I would see this weekend, I wanted to see hers the most. I sat beside her.

"Mrs. Torres, ma'am," I said.

She rolled her eyes and smiled, playfully slapping my wrist. "We've played too many hands for you to call me ma'am."

"I'm sorry, ma'am." I couldn't help myself; the sight of the autographed Jack of Spades in pieces on my bed made me grit my teeth. I didn't have the heart to tell her.

"And I told you to stop apologizing. You're like a damn broken record." Her voice was a bit more frail these days, but that Texas accent was still tough as shoe leather.

I slapped my forehead. "Yes, M...Ms. Enid." My Southern grandma would fly red eye to Las Vegas to put me over her knee if I dared to call this woman anything different. I wasn't ready want to test that theory.

"How the hell are you?"

I saw the signature hot pink dress out of the corner of my eye. Expensive-looking and tailored to fit, no doubt. A skinny black belt nipped grown woman hips at the waist. Toned legs caressed the bottom of her dress as she walked. Peek toe pumps. A wide-brimmed black hat hid her face, but I'd recognize my nemesis anywhere. She insisted on dressing like a cartoon villain today, apparently.

"Hot as hell," I said, absently. I meant the weather. Not Cruella over there.

She slithered toward us.

I tried to keep my face blank, but my teeth pinched my bottom lip anyway. If there's anything I took away from the hands I'd had played with her over the years, it was that I didn't like her. I didn't like playing with her. Enid had bad experiences with Miri Black at previous tournaments as well. While Enid was too much of a professional to play on tilt, Miri seemed to delight in tipping the boat just enough.

"Hey, ladies," Miri cooed, smirking at us. "Ready for another tournament?"

Enid pointedly ignored the question with a forced smile. The woman had zero tolerance for bullshit. Miri wouldn't get the pleasure of getting to me, not today. "Very much so," I said. "It's nice to see you again."

"I'm surprised you entered this tournament, Jax. I know how much you prefer playing with the boys." Miri pinned me in place with a grin. She had nice-nasty down to a science.

Me? I nearly spat. I'm not the one pushing my breasts up to distract the men at the table. That would have been below the belt, even for me. I tried diplomacy instead. "The guys have their shit, too." If this had been the sixties, I knew of two players who would've taken each other out back and busted up knee caps for the shit they talked to each other at the table. "I just play with folks who know the game."

"Ms. Poker. Always a pleasure." Enid's voice was cool, a taut thread in the hot, bustling room. A flash of forty-five caliber steel threaded through her voice. ""Little premature don't you think, you've only won a couple bracelets and now you're calling yourself that?" Her eyes crinkled, the corners of her mouth twitching into a grimace. About as warm as Buffalo in January. You could always tell when someone bit their tongue to keep from saying something else.

Miri tossed her long, dark hair over a shoulder, her grin wide and dangerous. A Ruger tucked into a garter belt. "If the Louboutin fits,

Enid," she returned, the word drawn out into a silky purr. "Still trying to play the old-fashioned way?"

Enid's smile didn't waver. She sat up straighter and motioned at Miri's signature, figure-hugging pink dress. "And you're still using your...charms, I see."

Miri's grin grew, flashing straight white teeth. "Whatever works."

Enid's gaze hardened, but her voice remained soft. "There's more to poker than just the play, Miri. It's about respect. Tradition."

Miri's response was a chuckle, low and throaty. "Oh, Enid. You and your *traditions*."

Embers sparked in Enid's eyes, a glimmer of the fire that must have burned red-hot in her younger days. Her lips pulled into a harder smile, and I bit back a smirk.

"Tradition has its place, Miri. So does respect." I nodded towards Enid as I spoke.

Miri's smile faded a bit, her gaze sharpening. "And so does winning."

"Indeed, it does," Enid said, the words heavy with unspoken meaning. "Indeed, it does."

Enid's dig amused me. She was too much of a lady to get down in the gutter with Miri, but at this point, she had nothing left to prove to anyone. She would retire as one of the greatest players of all time, no matter what. Maybe this last tournament meant enough to her, though, she was willing to get a little dirty.

"Good luck," I said, and I meant it. Day one was usually brutal. More than half of these players would be gone by tomorrow. I rocked back on my heels, ready to head to the tables, but I couldn't resist one last dig. "Hey, keep some chips off to the side for me, so I can take them from you later."

"You, too," Miri said, her smirk back in place. Baby pink nails smoothed the brim of her black hat, and she tipped it in my direction. The gesture reminded me of Kung Lao in *Mortal Kombat*, as if she was ready to fling it from her head and slice open my throat.

I shrugged it off, a thin smile on my lips. "I'll see you at the tables."

We walked away from each other and toward the poker room. I could feel Miri's eyes on my back, but I didn't turn around.

SHUFFLE UP AND DEAL

MIRI

The shuffle of cards and conversation filled the chilly air as I took my seat at the poker table. Women, sizing each other up behind black sunglasses, surrounded the faded green felt. I slid my buy-in receipt to the dealer and he pushed me my stack—10,000 in reds, yellows, and blues.

Smoothing my hair, I focused on the task at hand. Win this tournament and put Jax in her place. That smug grin of hers when she thought she had me beat last time still burned. She and her uppity mentor Enid with their pretentious talk of "decorum" and "tradition." As if wearing high collared shirts and suits and keeping your mouth shut was the only way for women to get respect at the poker table.

My aggressive style rattled them. The way I used my looks to throw opponents off balance. How I slammed big bets down with self-assurance. It wasn't "sweet." It wasn't soft.

Being sweet never won me a single pot, ever. I'm here to play hard and win. On my terms.

The conversation with Jax and Enid earlier kept playing back in my head. Enid going on about how my behavior damaged the reputation of women in poker. Jax standing there smirking, pretending to take the high road. Until I hit back.

"A true player keeps their emotions in check and respects the game," Enid had pulled me aside to say once. Like I'd asked for her damn opinion in the first place. As if my passion makes me less of a player. I wanted to wipe those smug smiles off their faces.

My fists clenched, thinking about it. This was my chance to show them up. I glanced around the room, eyeing potential rivals. Most were frumpy. Middle-aged with stern expressions. I wasn't worried. Once the cards started flying, their composure would crack. And I'd be there to pick up the pieces.

This was my table. My tournament. Time to stack some chips.

I took a deep breath and focused on the felt of the table, running my fingers along the smooth edges. The dealer shuffled the cards with a snap; the sound cut through the low murmurs around the room.

This was my element. Where I thrived. Not like those country club ladies Mama used to serve, sipping mint juleps at the 19th hole. The ones who clutched their pearls while their husbands looked down my dress in the cash games. Their withered, frowning lips pressed tight with judgment, only to frown when I walked off with the same cash they laid on their backs to make.

Well doubt this, I thought, and stacked my chip towers high. Their disapproving glances only fueled me more. Especially Enid, with her matronly pearls and pressed collars. The way her mouth pinched every time I sat down at her table, my Louboutin heels clicking on the floor.

She played dainty, folding at the slightest sign of trouble. That wasn't my style. I came to dominate. To stare down people twice my age and send them packing. The bigger the bet, the more I relished it.

I wanted to see the sweat beading on their foreheads when I pushed in my stacks.

Sure, it rubbed some people the wrong way. They called me reckless, impulsive. But I was calculating every move, assessing every tell. Just because I had fun doing it didn't make me any less of a player.

This tournament was my chance to prove it once and for all. To show them underestimating me was a mistake they'd regret. I glanced across the room and spotted some player watching me, whispering to the player next to her.

Whatever.

Absentmindedly, I shuffled my chips, going over my strategy again. Most of these players were unknowns—middle-aged women still chasing a tournament win or college kids hoping to be the next hotshot poker stars. Easy pickings.

Then there was Jax.

Cool, calculating Jax with her expensive watches and tailored vests.

Some things never change. Jax waltzed in with Enid practically fawning over her. Teacher's pet. Enid always had a soft spot for the ones who played by the rules. Jax gave me a curt nod, then took the seat directly across from me.

I wasn't going to let her icy demeanor rattle me. As the dealer began shuffling cards into play, I made sure to hold her gaze.

"See something you like?"

"That stack of chips in front of you might look good next to mine," I said.

Jax let out a short, derisive laugh. "Still as cocky as ever, I see."

I leaned back in my chair and regarded her coolly. "I prefer 'confident.' But I can understand why you'd confuse the two."

Jax's eyes narrowed slightly. Good—I'd gotten under her skin. The dealer finished shuffling and dealt the cards. I kept my expression neutral as I assessed my hand. Not great, but workable.

"So what's your plan?" Jax asked while rearranging her hole cards. "Bat your eyelashes and hope some fool goes easy on you?"

I smirked. "Oh, you know me better than that. I don't need any tricks to wipe the floor with you."

"Is that right?" Jax's voice was low, dangerous. The other players glanced nervously between us. Our rivalry was infamous on the circuit.

"That's right," I replied evenly. "But don't worry, darling, I'll try not to embarrass you too badly in front of Enid."

Jax clenched her jaw. I'd struck another nerve. The dealer cleared their throat, ready to begin play. Jax and I never broke eye contact. The gauntlet had been thrown down. Now it was time to play.

I kept my posture relaxed and my gaze steady as the first round of betting begun. Inside, though, my thoughts raced.

Jax and I had been rivals since we were both young upstarts trying to break into the pro circuit. She resented me for refusing to kiss up to the old guard like she did. I didn't care—respect was earned at the tables, not by brown-nosing.

Now here we were, facing off yet again. Jax acted so superior, but I knew she was intimidated by me. Why else would she feel the need to try to get under my skin before play even started? She was hoping to rattle me, get me off my game. It would not work.

I made a modest bet and waited for Jax's response. Guess my comment got under her skin. Pity. She raised aggressively, never breaking eye contact. Fine by me. She could play herself on tilt right out of this tournament.

A muscle in her jaw twitched when I calmly matched her bet. She was used to opponents folding when she pulled these power moves, like she wouldn't fold if someone bullied her right back. I wasn't so easily cowed.

The rest of the table got out of our way as the raising war escalated. It was just Jax and me now, staring each other down across the faded felt. I reveled in the challenge. Let her underestimate me—I would have the last laugh.

When the dust settled, I raked in the sizable pot. Jax's expression hardened.

"This game is just getting interesting. I do hope you'll stay and play." I winked and allowed myself a small, satisfied smile before turning my attention back to the cards.

It visibly frustrated Jax when I took down yet another pot. Good. Her emotions were getting the better of her. Meanwhile, I remained cool as a fan.

She seethed while I played more aggressively, raising and re-raising with reckless abandon. I bided my time, switching up by folding marginal hands to throw her off my game. Let her stew while the stats she ran in her head kept giving her the wrong answer.

The opportunity came a few hands later when I was dealt pocket Queens. My favorite hand. Jax raised in early position and I re-raised, forcing out the other players. She stared at me for a long moment, then tossed her cards into the pot.

Scaredy cat.

HEADS UP

JAX

It's very easy to tell who got good playing poker online, and the people who were used to playing in person. The internet players, they wore hoodies with sunglasses as big as their face, and spent the hands they weren't in looking at their phones. I preferred the old heads who came up in home games and casinos. Even if the table didn't have a motormouth to keep the mood light, it was always a good idea to know the people you're playing with. Learn their quirks.

Take Carol, for instance. A conservative player, she could be pushed out of a good hand. But if she rubbed the back of her salt and pepper hair as she called your bluff, you had better believe she's holding the nuts. Enid almost always saw the first round of bets, but she switched it up often. She could have nothing and pin you with a look until you mucked your hand, or she ducked out quickly. Miri was a Mack truck when she got good cards, but a smile and a hair toss never left you feeling like she had completely run you over with pocket fours.

Watching Miri play with the boys was always interesting. Baby pink nails and plump lips always left them confused whether she wanted their chips, or something else. When the wives watched the action from the gallery, they seemed to watch her as much as their own husbands. From the looks of them afterwards, it was usually the boys left the table wanting that something else. Quiet as it's kept, the circuit loved gossip. They were about as messy as those reality shows where women in sparkly designer gowns tore into each other with tongues as sharp as their nails. Oddly enough, no one had ever heard of Miri getting into any entanglements. I hadn't, anyway.

Personally, I didn't like the way she played. She was better at reading people than me, so I always had to switch up my style with her. Not that it even mattered at times; I could be bluffing, and she didn't even blink as she splashed the pot.

The sound of the dealer shuffling the glossy deck of cards brought me back to the present. The cards danced into place under her deft fingers, and I couldn't help but smirk. It was the sound of possibility, of the chance or winning, or being tossed out on your ass for a bad call. I both loved it and had a healthy fear of it.

On the small blind, I pushed a small stack towards the middle of the table.

Miri took a swig of designer water with strawberries and kiwi floating inside the bottle and tossed her chips onto the felt right on top of mine. The dealer shot cards across the felt to the players. Everyone at the table took turns peeking at and chucking away hole cards they didn't like, and the social media starlet who had been staring into her phone on every hand she mucked finally noticed. On the button, this was worth a shot.

"Twenty five hundred," she said. The shaky tap on the cards was a tell, clear as day. The sort of thing you'd see from a player who had probably just landed a lukewarm pair on the button in a hand with no callers. No better than my suited Spades, surely. But she had underestimated who was sitting two people to her left. On the small blind, I had to put up the bet, but wasn't committed any further than the flop.

To my left, Miri sat up and her gaze narrowed sharply on The Starlet like a camera zooming in on its subject. More like a hawk spotting its dinner. She picked more chips to splash into the pot for the re-raise.

Well, this should be interesting. My skin prickled pins and needles as the dealer burned the first card of the deck, sliding it out of play. Here we go.

Immediately, the dealer turned over the flop. As I thought, it was no help to me or my Spades, so I tossed back the Spades. I didn't need to be a hero. Almost through day one, the room already felt thinner. Less cramped. Less scents fighting for air space. The chatter at the tables turned all the way down. A quarter of the tables in the room were empty, others lopsided.

Nobody wants that moment where the camera zooms in as they stand up with what feels like a hot hand, only to watch it go bust on the turn or the river. I wasn't looking for that moment today.

"Well, that's no fun," Miri said.

I rolled my eyes. Was I the dinner? Why was I always the one she went after?

Across from us, Carol said nothing, but her eyes crinkled with something as she looked back and forth between Miri and me. Wonder what that look was about.

Another round of betting and, for a moment you could hear, as Grandma used to say, a mouse pissing on cotton.

Miri looked right through me to her, perfectly manicured eyebrows arched. She tapped the table wordlessly.

I smelled a trap. She was a bull stomping through fine china when she had something good, but she knew when to tiptoe when she had the nuts. Textbook bluff. The Starlet, well, she'd have to learn on her own.

A quick peek next to me showed The Starlet in deep concentration. Nobody spoke. Her lips moved slightly. Probably running stats, probabilities. Outs. The only other sounds in the room were dealers at other tables flipping over cards, and anxious players fiddling with their chips.

"Don't strain your brain too much, puddin'," Carol quipped, breaking the muted hum. "It's just poker."

Her calculations complete, The Starlet pushed two chip stacks into the pot. It looked like she was ready to take a stand. "Raise." The bet was so large it seemed like she was daring Miri to call.

My eyebrows shot up in surprise. She had guts, this one. The Starlet was pushing her luck, making a bet that screamed of desperation. Or overconfidence. Reminded me of the first time I was fresh off the online poker rooms and tried to bluff my way through a hand with nothing but high cards. I forgot people could see me, too. Got laughed out of the cash game.

From the patch crudely slapped into her shirt, she was playing with someone else's money anyway. Corporate sponsorship must be nice.

I took a quick sip of water to swallow any comments. No matter what you see on TV, talking over a hand you're not playing in is rude. You wouldn't want anyone chattering on about their family trip to Nowhere, PA while you're trying to focus, right?

The turn came, and of course it was a Spade. A kick right square in the teeth, because it wouldn't have helped me one bit.

Miri was up next.

Now, you can usually tell when someone is unsure about their hand. They sit up straight. They look unblinking at their opponent; they lift their hole cards for a second—or third—look. Miri didn't move an inch. She smoothly pushed all her chips into the center of the felt. "Raise."

To call that bet would put The Starlet all in.

"Ooh, shit!" Carol said. From the other side of the table, her laugh caught and deepened to a rasping nicotine bark. Thin wrinkled lips sucked in tight like she was about to take a drag from a cigarette.

Looking at her meager stack, she barely had enough chips to make the next blind bet. The Starlet's face dropped into a deep frown. No doubt, beating herself up for her grave miscalculation, same as I would've done. This was probably her last stand. Looking at her, I could only see a double rainbow hologram of myself in her mirrored sunglasses. She stood up, broad shoulders slumped over the felt, and flipped over her cards. "Let's go."

Miri stayed seated and tossed long, dark hair over her shoulder. Giggling, she had the good grace to look...sheepish? Bimbo mode activated. "You're going to hate me," she said.

Going to?

She turned her cards face up, real delicately, like she was handling a bomb. Everyone stared at her cards, and you could hear a stunned gasp run through the table. Even some of the women at the other table turned around to watch.

All this for a lowly pair of threes.

The dealer flipped over the last card. Six of Diamonds. Surveying the board, I shook my head in amazement. Huh. A single card could change anything on a dime, couldn't it? I could've made a back door straight, if I had stayed in the hand after all. Dammit. If I had called, it could have been me watching Miri trying to gather tight-lipped dignity as tournament security escorted her out.

The Starlet had gone all in with a high card, only to be taken out with a pair of threes. She stood at the table, white-knuckled fists digging into her hips until a balding gray-jacket came up from behind to walk her off the tournament floor.

That wasn't a bad beat, it was a stupid one. I was ticked for her.

The head gray-jacket guy, the director, came up to the table with him. He leaned over to speak to the dealer. Thankfully, some of us were going to fill out the other tables.

"Bass, table 10," he said. "Black, table 7..."

Miri took a delicate sip from her fruity water bottle. "Later, Jax."

"Hopefully much later, Miri," I said, refusing to break count to look at her.

"Final table work for you?" She couldn't take that annoying ass cocky purr out of her voice for even a second, could she? I ground my teeth as I stood up to walk away from the table.

Carol tapped the felt impatiently. "Get a room."

BABYGIRL

MIRI

The river card flashed, and my gut twisted. Enid flipped her hand—a full house. I stared at my three of a kind in disbelief as the room erupted in cheers and murmurs. Enid's eyes held mine, glinting with victory and worse—pity.

Fuck her, and fuck her pity.

"One hour lunch break, ladies. Be back promptly to continue," the director announced.

My chair screeched back. I couldn't breathe in here.

I had to get out. I shoved away my cards and quickly grabbed my purse, desperate for fresh air without pitying gazes boring into me. Jax's eyes collided with mine as I made my way to the exit. There was something there I couldn't quite name—surprise? Concern? Probably more of that fucking pity I never asked anyone for.

I pushed those thoughts away and shuffled out of the room. My steps hastened as I stalked down the long hallway, passing the neon sign that illuminated the poker room entrance.

I headed straight for the elevator, stabbing at the button. As soon as the doors slid shut, I slumped against the wall and closed my eyes. I could still feel Enid's gaze burning into me. So smug. So superior. She thought her style made her better than me somehow.

Alone inside, I sagged against the wall as the floors ticked by. When I stepped onto the patio outside my penthouse suite, the sights and sounds of the Strip washed over me. Tranquil and chaotic all at once. I sucked in a deep breath, willing the desert air to cleanse me.

Enid's pitying glance swam in my mind, mingling with old memories. My mother, head bowed, serving cocktails at the country club she could never join. My grandma, snubbed and talked about by the church Motherboard for her work at the brothel. Me—judged and dismissed in this world for my looks, my style. For daring to be feminine in their boys' club.

I thought Jax would understand. But she bought into their rules, too, like Enid. Never shook tables. With her pressed suits and status watches, she could pass for one of them.

Anger simmered in my gut. I wouldn't change who I was. Not for them, not for anyone. My family had endured far worse than scornful glances.

I leaned against the railing, staring out at the neon spectacle below. What did I expect from Jax, anyway? Kindred spirits? Understanding?

No. I didn't need anyone's understanding or approval. All I needed was the one thing I'd always had—myself.

My mind wandered back to late nights with Grandma Rose, playing cards at a rickety table in the back room of the brothel. She taught me cards weren't just a game. They were a skill, an art. A means to take control of your own destiny.

"Never depend on nobody but you, babygirl," she'd say, her gold tooth glinting when she grinned. "You make your own luck in this world."

I smiled thinking of her now. She'd get a kick out of watching me play, wearing Chanel and five-inch red bottom heels while I took down CEOs and lawyers.

When I walked back through those doors, I wouldn't be seeking anyone's approval. I'd be taking what was mine. And I'd do it my way.

I gritted my teeth and made my way back into the lobby. The clacking of my heels echoed off the walls, making me feel even more exposed than before. All around the room were screens playing footage from today's games—Jax and I competing against each other on a loop.

We had seemed so different side by side: her in her crisp button down, twisted locs pinned back in rows of braids; me in a curve-hugging dress, lips curved up slightly at the edges. But beneath it all, we shared something in common; we'd both had to fight to prove ourselves in the boys' club.

Still, it was hard for me to watch Jax lean back in her chair with confidence, raking in her chips. Even worse was the hint of a smile that lit up her eyes. She reveled in the game as much as I did—although she kept it hidden better than I ever could.

My jaw tightened as I watched her, determination firing through my veins like electricity. There was no way I gave a damn about winning her approval—but at the same time, I couldn't deny part of me wanted to go up against her again. Leave her with no choice but to respect me.

Next round, things would be different. I'd play my game, but with an edge she wouldn't expect. No one was knocking me out of this tournament. Not Enid, not Jax. No one.

I smirked, ready for the next hand.

DO IT IN MY NAME

JAX

A s much as it was an honor to play with the woman who taught me poker, it was also intimidating, too. I spent hours watching videos, studying her moves. Ms. Enid rarely cracked a smile at the table, but when she did, it was because someone had her beat. It was usually Minnie Chow, because they teased each other in the way only old friends could. Like watching Julia and Jacques in the kitchen as a kid.

Truth be told, I'd probably give up the tip of a pinky toe to hear a story of the two of them tearing up the Strip together.

Rare as her smile was, it was virtually non-existent now. When a familiar figure approaching the table, her sun-weathered mouth turned completely dour.

"Afternoon, ladies, it's a pleasure." Miri said, with a wave. "Jax."

Really? Was that necessary?

A gray tournament suit directed Miri towards an empty chair, right next to Ms. Enid.

When Miri sat down and took her place, I caught Ms. Enid pressing her lips together. She looked away to chat with Carol. Miri, seeing the snub, smiled tightly at the rest of the players at the table. Upon spotting me, Miri looked me up and down, and then turned to the player next to her, a little too quickly.

Whatever that was about, I almost shot back, *the feeling's mutual.*

After a round of chip counts, the dealer set the dealer button in front of me, and shuffled her cards.

"Let's get it." I tapped the felt. The first round of cards hit the table expertly, efficiently. When the dealer slid the second round of cards, I sat up. Peeked underneath my hand.

Nine-Seven, off suit. I didn't like it, but it was worth something. Pairs, trips, or a straight, but not much good for anything else. Only Miri and Enid placed bets before me. The other ladies quickly tossed their cards back, uninterested. The Small Blind tucked her cards under French-tipped manicured nails.

She was staying in the hand.

The Big Blind stayed in, too.

I didn't really like going five-handed into a round, but the flop had a way of thinning out the herd real quick.

The dealer burned the first card, and then flipped over the flop. Two, Three, Five.

Ms. Enid gave away nothing. Looking at her face would never, ever reveal her hand. "Call."

Had Miri even bothered to look at her cards? Too busy looking at me instead. "Raise," she said. "Twenty-five hundred."

Other players waited for the flop to squeeze people out of play, Miri gleefully did the squeezing. It was as if you could see pulp and seeds dripping from her fingers.

Back to me.

Crunch time, Bass. I sat forward. Was this something worth fighting for? Maybe, at the final table, it might be. But, was it worth it right now?

Was I letting her do exactly what she was trying to do, getting underneath my skin?

Decisions, decisions. I played with two chips in my hand, sliding them back and forth on top of each other.

Let someone push you around once, and they keep doing it again and again until you push back harder.

She wasn't going to bully me out of this hand like she did ole girl yesterday. "Raise. Four thousand."

"Well, look at this." Miri's eyebrows shot up as she looked around the table. Coral pink lips curved into a smirk and she looked at me with an amused glint in her eyes. "Someone came to play today, ladies."

I quickly peeked down the table. Small Blind tossed her cards back into the center of the table, disgusted with whatever she had. The Big Blind followed suit.

Me, Ms. Enid and Miri. Three-handed, now.

The dealer played the next card. Eight.

Now it was me sitting on the edge of a gut shot straight. Still needed a six to complete the set. This was as close as I liked to cut it.

Ms. Enid checked, a curt nod of her head.

Miri smiled wider and continued the bets. "I call your four thousand, and raise another five."

Too Goddamn much. Too high of stakes for this hand and too risky for me to continue. My pride wanted me to take her down.

Pride also had me locked up in a hand I had no fucking business being in, this late. Better to lick my wounds and try another day.

I looked at my chip stack. I had enough for another five rounds before I was toast. Whatever victory Miri was celebrating, it was hers. She could have it. For now.

I slowly pushed my chips back into the pot and threw my cards into the muck pile with a shake of my head. "Fold."

Miri's eyes lit up with triumph. She already knew her victory was assured and leaned back in her chair, looking smugly at Ms. Enid. "Well, what do you have?"

A straight, probably. I don't dare say it out loud. Even if it were legal in tournament poker, I'd cut my own tongue out before I helped Miri.

The older woman ignored Miri. She gestured to the dealer to draw the next card. "Let's get on with it."

Nine of Clubs. Would have given me a pair, which would have been squashed real quick by whatever Ms. Enid was sitting on.

Ms. Enid cast an icy glare over the table before finally turning her gaze to Miri. Her voice was cold and unwavering when she spoke. "Raise, six thousand."

Carol turned to Ms. Enid. "You know, Enid, the point here is to win chips, not lose 'em."

Miri swiveled toward Ms. Enid. "You must have a great hand, Enid." She leaned in like she was sharing a secret. "I promise you mine is better."

Ms. Enid sneered. "Put up then, buttercup. Quit your yapping."

Miri chewed it over. In all the time I've played with her, only a handful have ever had the guts to try to bully Miri out of a hand.

Ms. Enid was bullying the bully.

Still eyeing Ms. Enid, Miri pushed all of her chips into the center of the felt. "All in."

The crowd gasped. Even Carol looked a bit taken aback.

The cameraman came over and zoomed in on our table.

Ms. Enid had made her straight on the flop, with Five high.

Miri had made hers on the river, with the Nine delivering the final blow.

My shoulders deflated. Ms. Enid was going to retire without her bracelet this year.

As a kid, I watched a graying, steel-eyed Enid Torres stare down Piotr Mazur and his suited Jack-Ten until he tossed the cards on the felt, muttering.

Today, she was more gracious in defeat, going around the table to shake hands with everyone on her way out. The people sitting in the spectator gallery applauded her as she waved at them from the platform.

For the first time ever, she looked frail to me. My hero was just a woman, after all.

Ms. Enid paused at Miri's chair, looking like she was about to say something, but thought differently of it. Miri didn't stop counting her chip stack long enough to acknowledge her.

When she reached me, Ms. Enid leaned in. I pressed a firm hand over the mic so the audience couldn't hear. "Take her down for me," she said, and patted me on the shoulder.

I looked up at her and laughed in surprise. "With pleasure."

Seven o'clock. The same time some people are picking out which wine to have with dinner, and we're still playing hands. Two more women followed Enid out the door shortly after. One I took out with a monster bluff. Miri crushed some online prodigy's hopes with pocket Queens.

This hand, I slapped down Six-Ten off suit. I was nowhere near the button, and we were wrapping up play for the night. Tomorrow was another day.

Miri smiled at her cards. "You're smarter than I give you credit for."

I glared at Miri. That smug, self-satisfied smirk of hers could grind gravel to dust.

Carol rolled her eyes. "If you two are done eye-fucking each other, some of us are here to play poker."

"What's your problem, Carol?" I asked. "You've been riding my ass all day."

"Maybe if you stopped disrupting the game every other hand to bicker with Miri, I wouldn't have to," Carol snapped. She slapped her hand down on the small stack of coins when she said it, sending a $100 coin rolling into the pot. The dealer looked towards the tournament director.

Miri shrugged. "What can I say? She brings out the worst in me." She wouldn't look at me, though, as she said it. Her cheeks flushed a deep red.

"Feeling's mutual, Miri," I muttered, rubbing the back of my neck.

Carol rolled her eyes. "Look, even my kid has balls enough to tell a girl he likes her! So why don't you just get a room and work it out, so the rest of us can play in peace?"

The TV Chef's eyebrows rose over the brim of her oversized Balenciaga glasses.

Turning to the dealer, Carol shoved her collapsed stack to the middle of the table. "All in."

I looked around; the cameras were elsewhere at the moment. Shera Morales looked back and forth between us, with barely repressed amusement.

Miri looked at her chips like she wanted to fling them at someone. Carol? Me? Who knows. She glanced at Carol. "How many chips do you have?"

Carol had done something I hadn't: getting Miri to play on tilt. Not that I hadn't tried, but Miri always gave back as good as she got, smirked and played the hand as if I hadn't spoken at all.

The dealer counted the chips. I tapped the felt, impatient. Dammit. If anyone was going to take Miri out, I wanted to be the one to do it. For Enid. For the satisfaction of seeing her and her designer bags sulking off the floor and out of my face until the next tournament.

"Twenty thousand, five hundred," the dealer said.

Miri looked at her cards, then at Carol's chips. "I call."

The whole table froze, suddenly interested. The TV Chef pulled her glasses down as she leaned in.

"Fine," Carol said, turning her cards up. Seven-Ten of Diamonds. "Let's see what you've got."

Wordlessly, Miri turned over her cards.

The dealer flipped over the turn: a Club. Miri had the Ten-Jack of Clubs, giving her a flush. Carol could still get a gutshot Eight, but if the Eight was a Club, Carol was done. The other players groaned when that's exactly what came up.

I winced as the dealer turned over the Two of Clubs, making Miri's hand complete. A kick in the teeth at this point.

"Shit," I said, leaning back in my chair. The dealer pushed the pot towards Miri. At least none of mine were in there.

Miri's smile curled into the nastiest sneer as she looked me up and down. "Looks like you and I are stuck with each other a bit longer, huh?" For a split second, she looked like she might enjoy that. Would she?

"Oh, I don't mind that." I shoved my hands into my pockets to hide balled up fists. "Just gives me another chance to knock you out later."

Carol didn't know what the fuck she was talking about. Of course I didn't want Miri in that way, and she didn't want me. We just liked getting a rise out of each other, more than anyone else at the table.

"I'll take that as a compliment." Miri's voice was a low purr. "Though, I wouldn't want to be in your shoes when I beat you."

"Don't get ahead of yourself." I grinned, trying to look more confident than I felt."You're not getting this bracelet without a fight."

"Now, now, children," Carol said, as she got up from the table. "The rest of you ladies, enjoy your evening."

BITTER NOTES

MIRI

The fading sun cast long shadows across the cobblestone as I stared into my cooling espresso. My thoughts churned like the foam that had long since dissolved into the dark liquid.

I couldn't get Jax's face out of my mind—the tension in her jaw, the fire in her eyes as she watched her mentor Enid walk away. My victory should have felt sweeter, but instead it left an aftertaste as bitter as this espresso. I'd take it, anyway. It was long due after years of condescension from Enid.

Yet my satisfaction was tempered by the memory of Jax's cold stare, full of accusation. Were we not rivals, her gaze might have lit a fire in me of a different kind—one I dared not name.

"Oh my God, you're Miri!" a voice squealed, jolting me from my thoughts. I looked up to see a gaggle of young women surrounding my cafe table, eyes bright with awe.

One of the players, a slender redhead, gushed, "That match against Enid was epic! The way you baited her into going all-in? Masterful."

I smiled tightly, the compliment souring in my mouth. "Just part of the game."

The redhead nodded eagerly, her friends joining in to sing my praises. But then another player, a tall blonde, chimed in with an imitation of Enid's voice, mocking her for her conservative approach.

I felt my smile evaporate and my chest tighten at the disrespect. My feelings towards Enid were my own, but mama would've slapped the taste clear from her mouth for speaking like that about an elder, and mine for allowing it. She probably didn't mean it, but this kid mocking Enid was no better than the trolls online mocking me. "Enid and I have a...complex dynamic, let's say. That's no secret. But every player, every style has its place in this game," I admonished gently.

The girl froze and looked down sheepishly as the other players glanced between us nervously. I softened my tone and said, "Poker is not just about winning—it's also about learning from your opponents and appreciating everyone's gameplay. Right?"

The blonde nodded slowly before mumbling something about respecting elders and diverging philosophies.

"Don't tell Enid I said that, though. That's just between us girls." I winked at her to keep the mood light.

The shyest fan edged forward, eyes averted as she extended a sealed deck of cards and a black marker. "C-could I get an autograph?"

Despite myself, I was charmed. She had an innocence about her I had lost a long time ago. I scrawled a quick signature and posed for a selfie, eliciting squeals of delight.

As we said our goodbyes, the redhead added slyly, "Does Jax smell as good as she looks?" The shy one had the grace to look horrified, but the other girls dissolved into giggles.

Like bergamot and sandalwood, I almost said. I bit my tongue and instead forced a laugh, their teasing hitting too close. The sun slipped below the horizon, and I looked towards the casino, wondering how much longer I could resist confronting the tension between Jax and me.

I waved off their teasing with a practiced smirk, but inside my stomach churned. Their comments were a stark reminder of the constant scrutiny I was under. Spectators hungry for drama analyzed and dissected my every interaction with Jax. God knows what they were saying online. I didn't dare look.

Carol's annoyed comments cut me deeper than bone, through and through. That had been enough.

Part of me longed to confront Jax, to demand an explanation for the simmering tension between us. But a bigger part was afraid of what I might unleash. A fire smoldered beneath our rivalry, that much was clear. But stoking those flames could mean getting burned.

I tried to shake off the girls' goodnight wishes as I walked away, but their remarks stuck like glue in my mind. Thoughts of Jax consumed me, and with every passing moment, anxiety grew deeper than a festering wound. Did I dare try to resolve our issues? The very thought made my heart race with anticipation, yet I feared what the outcome may be. Was it better to let things remain unresolved?

As dusk deepened into night, I made my way back inside, questions swirling. Should I risk it all and lay myself bare before my rival? Or continue pretending the heat between us was only animosity? I had no answers, only a restless energy that would not let me sleep. Not until I'd spoken to her.

CANARY YELLOW

JAX

M iri and her low-cut canary yellow dress swayed up to the bar. Her breasts almost spilled right onto the counter, with only tanned brown arms to contain them. Ugh. Show off. The yellow lights bouncing off the different bottles was my distraction. Jameson, Smirnoff, Don Julio, Dark Horse, I read. Dark locs were piled high on her head, spilling down her shoulders.

Looking away quickly, I licked away the last drops of the pinkest cranberry vodka ever. Our bartender here poured heavier than a kettle bell.

"A whiskey sour for me, and please refill my good friend's drink," I heard her say. Three seats were open at the bar and, of course, Miri just happened to sit at the one right next to me. Of course. From the corner of my eye, I could see her looking at me. Onscreen, Rocio Velez tapped gloves with Delphine Desjardins and jogged backwards to her corner. Neither of them even blinked.

"Jax," Miri said. Was that supposed to be a greeting?

The yellow dress hugged her waist and stopped short of covering what could be some kind of tattoo on her left thigh. Not that I noticed any of that. I was still ticked about her taking out Enid. I cleared my throat. "*Miriam* Black. My good friend."

"My whole government name, huh?" When I didn't answer, Miri tried again. "Do you think Rocio's going to win this one?"

I was so not in the mood for this. We had been going back and forth all day at the table and now she wanted to make small talk? I glared at her. "What do you want?"

"To relax," she said, as the bartender set down our drinks. She clinked her glass against mine, flashing a predatory smile. "You're too wound up."

"I don't need your help relaxing," I spat.

"And I don't know why you insist on antagonizing me," Miri said, flipping her hair over her shoulder. "If you think I can't beat you, why do you look so tense right now?"

"You, beat me? Not gonna happen," I scoffed. "If you spent less time batting your eyelashes at the boys and more time practicing your poker, maybe then you'd have a chance at beating me."

"Ah, so that's really what you think of me," Miri said, taking a sip of the whiskey sour. "I won two bracelets by flirting. Not with skill, or reading people, or anything. Just showing my tits. How many have you won again?"

Ouch. I went silent for a moment, swallowing the pink drink. A splash more cranberry this time. Maybe I might have been behaving unfairly toward Miri. "You're right," I said finally. "You've won more than me. But that's going to change tomorrow."

"Oh, I'm not so sure about that," Miri said, with a smile. Maybe it was the alcohol, but her cheeks bloomed, rose soft. "You might need to rethink that if you keep playing Ten-Two, off suit."

Touché. If anything, Miri was a master at disarming people. Pat Arnold's been a whole puppy since she expertly deflected his assertion that she was holding pocket tens only to lay them down when he went all in.

How many times have I seen this before? Miri looking up at men through her lashes because she knew they couldn't tell if she was bluffing or not. She could be holding pocket aces or junk, and you wouldn't care. The rush of blood leaving the head at once does that, I guess.

Our bartender came back with our bill. Without thinking, I reached into my pocket to pull out my card. When the server brought out the check, Dru would always be in the ladies' room or pretend to be busy until I pulled out my card, even if she had offered to pay earlier that evening. I hope she's having fun paying for everything on her own.

Miri tapped me on the arm, and it was fucking electric. My wrist felt all weird and hot. Wasn't expecting that.

"I invited myself," Miri said, with a quick nod to my wallet. "Put that away."

Excuse *me*.

We watched the match in silence, for the most part, except for when Rocio locked her forearm around Delphine's head and squeezed, even as the woman's face went deep red. As her arm went limp, the ref called it. Rocio released the clutch immediately, revealing a ring of stark white around Delphine's neck. Holy shit.

"Do you think Carol's right about what she said? About you and me?" Miri's voice was throaty and low, her hand curling around my wrist. No longer looking at me from the side, she was facing me directly. She was like Russell Winbrook in third grade, who had liked tugging at my ponytails because he liked me.

"Carol is twice-divorced and pays her ex-wife alimony," I said.

"I see the way you look at me," Miri said. She crossed her legs and I got a better look at the thigh tattoo. Something floral. It looked raised. Fresh. Wonder if I could make her squirm the same way she made me, just by tracing a finger up the raised curve.

Jesus help me.

Again, I wasn't looking. I swear. I loosened up the neck of my shirt. Certainly, it must've been the drinks making me feel a little too warm.

"How is that different from how everyone looks at you?" I asked.

Miri picked the cherry out of her drink and rolled it between her red lips before she took it into her mouth. She smiled and walked fingers up my arm. "How's that, exactly?"

"With barely contained lust." My eyes drift down to parted red lips, and then quickly back to the screen. She would get no epiphanies from me today.

People crowded around the bar as Rocio's handlers lifted her hands in victory with the gold belt.

More ice. I needed more ice. It wasn't even warm anymore; it was uncomfortable. Suffocating and hot. Like, I could get up now but would have to press against her to pass through. Feeling Miri's body against mine was the last thing I needed right now, yet it was also all I wanted right then. I knew she knew this. I knew she wanted this, too. My gut tightened in response. The anger from this morning was back, so hard it made my leg jump.

That's what this is. Anger. Not the need to snatch her by the waist and pull her into my lap, not at all.

Sitting across from her all day sounds like hell. Except, it feels different now. Fuck Carol.

I tried to ignore the way my body was responding to her touch. Instead, I focused on the annoyance that had been simmering inside me all day. "We're not doing this, Miri." My voice was clipped; cold. I'd had about enough of her games. "I won't be your experiment."

Miri pouted, but she didn't back away. Instead, she pressed closer, running her hands up the seam of my pants until they were sitting at my zipper. What would it feel like with her fingers touching me underneath? Glaring, I throbbed in response.

I tried to step back, but she held me in place. Looked me dead in the eye. "I'm calling your bluff, Jax."

"Carol was just trying to get a rise out of us," I said. The way my heart sped up said was lying.

Miri slammed back the whiskey sour, looking me in the eye the whole time. "What's the harm in finding out? If she's wrong, she's wrong."

I damn near sprinted for the exit.

"See you at the tables." I couldn't get out of there fast enough. "Goodnight, Miri."

RIPPLES AREN'T JUST CHIPS

MIRI

The brown liquor burned my throat as I took another sip. The bartender's eyes followed me closely, like a hawk circling its prey.

"Rough night, huh?" He said, breaking the silence.

I nodded, not offering more. I wasn't in the mood for small talk, especially not with a stranger.

"I saw you play earlier. That was one hell of a game."

"Thank you." I managed a tight smile in response. He was fishing, but I wasn't biting.

"You know, poker is a lot like life. Full of highs and lows. Wins and losses." He continued, ignoring my closed-off body language. What did he think this was? *Cheers?*

"I'll take another one of these." I swirled the whiskey in my glass, watching the ice cubes chase each other in half-circles. A pointless exercise, destined to go nowhere. Much like this conversation.

"I think you've had enough for tonight," he said, finally, his voice firm but not unkind as he slid the check toward me. Message received.

I didn't argue. I was too raw, too exposed sitting here under the weight of his assessing gaze. I pulled out a few bills, not bothering to count them, and dropped them on the bar.

"Keep the change," I muttered, grabbing my clutch and sliding off the stool.

The bar's pulsing music and stuffy air now felt suffocating. I needed some fresh air. As I turned to leave, I remembered the rooftop pool the bellhop had mentioned earlier. Perfect.

As I made my way across the lobby, the click of my heels on the tile echoed through the empty corridors. The shadows leaned in, closing around me. I felt caged, trapped by my circling thoughts.

I quickened my pace.

The day's events replayed in my mind on an endless loop. What had I been thinking, coming on to Jax like that? I was usually more controlled, keeping my cards close to my chest.

Women weren't like cards. I didn't chase women; they chased me.

But something about her broke through my typical restraint.

When I stepped out into the night, the view momentarily stunned me. The lights of the city stretched to the horizon, a sea of glittering possibility.

I slipped off my heels, and sat down, letting my feet sink into the cool water of the pool. The soft ripples soothed my skin.

Out here, surrounded by the hushed darkness, I could almost pretend I was alone. No one watching me or judging me. Just me and the stillness of the night.

I let out a long exhale, feeling some of the tension leave my shoulders. The cool night air caressed my skin as I splashed at the water, trailing my fingers along the edge of the pool before getting up again.

The faint sound of traffic drifted up from the streets below. Otherwise, it was quiet. Peaceful. My mind started to settle, calming the chaotic swirl of emotions.

I found a lounge chair tucked away in a shadowy corner and sank down onto it with a sigh. The cushion embraced me when I leaned back. Tilting my face up to the ink blue sky, I could see a few stars glimmered faintly through the city haze. A plane dipped lower in the sky, headed for the airport at the end of the Strip.

What was I doing here? I'd gotten caught up in the momentum of the game, let my competitiveness override my better judgment. Now here I was, hiding on a rooftop to avoid facing the mess I'd made.

Maybe I should leave. The minute I got my bracelet, or surrendered the last of my chips, get on the first flight back to San Diego, and put this whole disaster of a tournament behind me.

But even as the thought crossed my mind, I knew I wouldn't.

I'd never walked away from a challenge in my life because Mama didn't raise a quitter. And she certainly didn't raise me to hand over two million bucks without one hell of a fight.

A wry smile twisted my lips.

The misstep earlier had revealed my own vulnerabilities, my desire for her. But it also exposed something in Jax—a hunger she tried to mask. Perhaps she'd given me another weapon in my arsenal to use against her, or at least something to replay in my mind as I tried to sleep tonight. It ticked at me I didn't know which one it was. Which one I wanted it to be.

My own damn fault.

The sound of the access door opening broke the stillness. I tensed, wondering if Jax had somehow found me. But the footsteps receded without approaching. Whoever it was hadn't noticed me tucked away in the shadows. The door shut behind them.

Alone again. I took a deep breath and closed my eyes. I would face Jax tomorrow, this time with my armor intact. For now, I would enjoy this moment of solitude the best way I could.

I slipped off my heels and dipped my feet into the pool, savoring the cool water on my skin. Tiny ripples spread out from my toes, breaking the stillness of the surface.

Like my life lately—calm one moment, chaotic the next. Ever since Jax had swaggered into that tournament room, I'd been off balance, reacting instead of acting. Well, no more.

Tomorrow I'd take back control. Deal myself a better hand. I needed to get through tonight first.

I took a few more deep breaths, letting the tension ease from my shoulders. The breeze lifted a curl against my cheek in a soft caress.

In the distance, cheers and music rumbled up from the street as cars whizzed by. The city pulsed with frenetic energy even at this late hour, oblivious to my inner turmoil.

Part of me yearned to lose myself in that chaos and noise and avoid facing the mess I'd made tonight. The bigger part knew I had to face this. Had to face her.

I stood, water dripping from my feet to form small dark spots on the concrete. This moment of peace was an illusion. The real game was waiting for me behind my suite door, in my empty bed.

I headed back inside, ready to call it a night. As I walked down the quiet corridor towards my room, the sound of voices caught my attention. I glanced over to see a concierge talking to a familiar figure. Fucking Jax.

Even exhausted, she exuded magnetic energy I found intoxicating. Her strong shoulders sagged slightly as the concierge closed the door to the penthouse suite—right next to mine.

I couldn't help the smirk that crossed my face. What were the odds? To be a shit, I winked.

"Howdy, Neighbor."

ADVANCED HORNET'S NEST
KICKING TECHNIQUES

JAX

A lone, finally, in my own damn room.

I went to the bar to relax. Now I'm wound up even tighter than I was when I sat down at the tables. The throbbing tension in my pants was a whole nuisance when there's only a hand to work out that tension.

I locked the door behind me and stood there for a moment until my belly stopped coiling as tight as a spring. The door was a welcome coolness against my back.

Who the fuck does Miri think she is, Mae West? She can go live out her straight girl fantasies with someone else.

Miri probably thought she could saunter into a room and bring me to my knees in lust. All because Carol kicked over a hornet's nest. Flirting with someone just to feed her bottomless ego? Lower than I thought she could go. Anything to win, right? Fuck Carol. And fuck Miri, too.

Though I'm ready to blow my lid, I take a deep breath. My old shrink called it grounding. Something I can see, something I can smell, something I can hear. Anything right now to pull the tension from my thighs that doesn't involve getting between hers.

I smelled...flowers?

A look at the middle of the bed indeed showed a bouquet of flowers. The scent drew me across the room. A burst of bright colors, oranges, reds, calla lilies exploding from dark green stems. The woven basket had Tennessee whiskey. Dark chocolate pretzels, fat chocolate strawberries with white chocolate zigzagged across. I rifled through the basket, hearing the cellophane crinkle as I tore through it. Kale chips. Sweet Maui barbecue chips.

Someone's been doing their homework on me. Who sent these?

I snatched the card sticking out of the flower bunch.

You can't put a price on love, I read. *Love, D.*

"Oh, this is rich." I tossed the card back onto the bed. Did I pay for that, too? She's petty enough to send me something with my own money. The throbbing left my groin to shoot straight into my head. Ugh.

I'm *so* not in the mood for this. Snatching up the bedside phone, I dialed the front desk.

"Front Desk, Noelle," a voice chirped. "How may I help you?"

"Noelle, we have a problem. There was a basket left in my room. I didn't order anything."

The phone went quiet as Noelle typed something. "I'm showing here it was a gift from your wife?"

My teeth could've ground glass to dust at that moment. "Not married."

"I'm so sorry, Ms. Bass, I'm not sure how this happened. I'll have a manager look into this for you immediately! Please hold."

Noelle put me on hold as she contacted the manager.

After a few moments, I heard a male voice come through the line saying, "Ms. Bass, I apologize for this misunderstanding. We will do a full investigation, but can we move you to another room and offer you a complimentary gift basket for the inconvenience?"

Misunderstanding, my ass. All this was was my ex tap dancing on my last damn nerve an entire state away.

The whiskey in the basket was a temptation, but you couldn't pay me any amount of cash or chips to drink anything Dru sent. Yet, going back down to the bar for round two of Miri and that tight yellow dress would have me on full tilt. Tables were an early call, anyway. My days of playing hung over were long, long gone.

I sat down on the bed, rubbing my temples, and groaned as weariness set in. I was close to calling Noelle and her manager and telling them to cancel the room transfer so I could get some damn sleep, but before I knew it, they were at the door.

In a luxury hotel, the higher the room, the better the view. I knew when we had all stepped on the elevator going up, up, up, the room was going to be something serious.

The windows—bigger than the ones in my old room—set off incredible views of the Las Vegas strip. Neon lights, dancing lighted fountains, and billboards blocked out the mountains in the distance.

"If you ever tire of the view," the bellhop—Jim—said, "press this button." Gunmetal gray blackout curtains smoothly pulled shut.

I nodded, numb, taking in the mid-century-inspired space. My feet dragged across the carpet. The brass countertops had an industrial-sized espresso machine and an ice maker. Overlooking the living room part of the suite was an oversized black and white portrait of Dorothy Dandridge. Whoa.

Bill, the manager, piped up. "Is this room to your liking, Ms. Bass?"

At that point, a basement in the casino with dusty old slot machines and worn-out chairs would've sufficed, as long as it was quiet. This wasn't bad, though. I nodded.

"Should you need anything else," Bill said, handing me a card, "please call my direct number. We will sort this out."

"Thank you, Bill. I appreciate it. Now if you'll excuse me, it's been a long day." I motioned towards the door.

Bill smiled. "I hear ya. It was my pleasure, Ms. Bass. Good luck tomorrow!" Before he had closed the door entirely, a bounce of long curls and a yellow dress sauntered past my door.

No. It *can't* be.

To be sure, I went to the door and peeked out to see Miri opening her door. She turned to me with a wink.

"Howdy, Neighbor."

Fuck. Me.

RIVER FLUSH OR BUST

MIRI

The morning sun streamed in through the floor-to-ceiling windows, assaulting my eyes. I groaned and turned away, pulling a pillow over my head. The soft down did little to block out the light or the pounding in my temples. Must've forgotten to close the curtains last night. Too late to go back to sleep now.

I might have had to surrender to the day, but that didn't mean I had to be happy about it, either, especially after last night.

The plush carpet sank beneath my bare feet as I paced the spacious penthouse suite. Outside, the Vegas Strip looked slow and peaceful, a glaring contrast to the turmoil churning inside me.

I stared at the wall, heart racing as I remembered the lingering tension between Jax and me from last night. What was she doing on the other side? Was she reflecting on our encounter, too, or had it been forgotten in her sleep? I wished I could go to her, but instead I kept staring at the wall that separated us.

Maybe the wall between us was there for a reason. To keep us both from peeking over to the other side.

I was so, so irritated with myself. This wasn't like me, to be so thrown off by anyone. Especially not Jax.

So what, I'd gotten carried away pushing her buttons at the bar and watching her iceberg-cool composure crack. Seeing her flustered had thrilled me more than it should have.

The thrill of watching her eyes darken and her jaw clench from our closeness was as satisfying as a flush on the river.

I brushed my fingertips over the textured wallpaper, all that separated me from Jax. Did she realize how affected I'd been as well? How off balance she left me feeling, even now?

My phone chimed with a text message. I took a deep breath and turned away from the wall. Time to put last night behind us. I had a tournament to focus on. No more of this carrying on like a cheerleader with a crush.

I took a seat on the Chesterfield sofa and picked up my phone. Carol's text glowed again on the screen, inviting me to the group breakfast before the big tournament.

My stomach fluttered with anticipation mixed with dread. I'd have to face Jax again after our charged encounter at the bar.

I replayed every moment in my mind. Her look of shock when I first joined her at the bar. The sarcastic banter between us that held an undercurrent of something brimming right at the surface. Just waiting. How I'd boldly moved closer. My fingers grazing her arm. Her sharp intake of breath.

The thrill as I toyed with her, watching her falter and lose her composure, feeling her pulse race. It was a heady feeling, making the ice queen melt just a little.

But it was a dangerous game I played. I had revealed more of myself than intended. The subtle tremble in my own fingers when I touched her. The hitch in my breath when she held my gaze.

What if she had seen? My heart clenched. I couldn't let her know how affected I was, how vulnerable.

I set down the phone with a sigh. Perhaps I should keep away from Jax, at least until after the tournament. Beyond that, even. Focus on winning, not my tangled emotions. Put enough distance between us to forget this whole thing happened.

I stood and headed for the shower, steeling myself. Time to put on a game face and go join the others. And hope I didn't slip the moment I saw her again.

I stepped into the steaming shower, the hot water soothing my nerves. As rivulets streamed down my skin, my thoughts drifted unbidden to Jax in the room next door.

Was she also standing under a stream of water, bare skin slick with suds? Was she even slicker below, thinking about touching me? A tremor went through me at the image and I squeezed my thighs together. Abruptly, I shut off the water.

Get a grip, Miri. I toweled off roughly, determined to get the upper hand again. Jax may have gotten to me a little last night, but I wouldn't let it happen twice.

ON THE HOUSE

JAX

The next morning, my phone beat my alarm to the punch.

My room was quiet and dark. Money buys peace. The warmth from high-thread count sheets whispered sweet nothings to me in the cool room. I slapped away the angry button urging me out of bed. It was worth sacrificing a couple of big blinds to get an extra hour of sleep. How many times have I seen other players with a steaming paper coffee cup and a buttered poppy seed roll strolling in after the day's play had started? The thought lingered as my limbs relaxed, drifting back into sleep.

Not to be outdone, Ms. Enid's voice snatched me up real quick out of my dream. I shot up. The woman in it, who had a weird mix of Miri's disapproving glare and Dru's pout, probably would not be waiting for me if I drifted off again.

I looked at the phone in alarm, and immediately cleared my throat into something that hopefully would not sound like a growl. The display showed a live call on the other line. "Good Morning, Ms. Enid."

"Mornin', sunshine. I know you spent the night chasing the pretty young chicks, but did you forget you had a date with us old hens this morning?"

"No ma'am," I lied, rising out of bed.

"Now that's a crock of shit, and you know it," Ms. Enid laughed, her voice full of mischief. "We'll see you in a half."

I had already yanked off my night scarf, rushing towards the bathroom. "Yes ma'am. See you soon."

A whiff of some expensive cinnamon-smelling perfume floated from somewhere behind me. On God, I hated myself at that moment for knowing, feeling she was close by. Had my back stiff all the way up. "A rare sight indeed, Jax making nice with...people."

If this was what I had to endure for the next few days, I would gladly forfeit the rest of my chips. Just to never hear that self-satisfied purr she did when she thought she had one-upped me for the rest of this damn tournament.

"Miriam Black," I said, dropping my utensils onto the table. She wouldn't get the pleasure of seeing how hard I gripped the fork, not today. "To what do we owe the horror?"

"Now, darling, let's not say things we don't really mean. I'd hate to start the day on the wrong foot." Miri spoke like she was talking to a child. "Such a lovely spread—"

Now Ms. Enid looked uncomfortable, and a part of me sank. I could have slid under the table if no one would have noticed. "Ladies, can we just have a nice breakfast without the Jax and Miri show? For once?"

The smallest, pettiest part of me wanted to protest Miri had started with me this time. She was probably annoyed I turned her down last night.

I held my tongue, not wanting to give her any more satisfaction than she already had. Miri smiled, her eyes sparkling with amusement. "Oh, Enid. You know you love our little banter. It's just harmless fun."

Enid raised her eyebrows at me. I was in first grade, again, getting yoked up by the ears by my teacher all over again.

Fuck this. This was annoying, it was aggravating, but the last thing it was, was fun.

"So, what brings you here, bright and early?" Since we're bantering. Isn't that what she called it? "I know you like strolling in after play has begun."

"Jax," Carol warned. Now, *this* was like the auntie who walked off her job to come to pick you up for acting up at school.

"I do, usually. But I heard you were here and I just had to see for myself. It's not often we get a chance to see Jax away from the boys' club." Miri winked at the waiter who had pulled out her chair for her.

Ms. Enid cut into a plate of cooling scrambled eggs harder than she needed to. "Nothing worse than cold grits, Jax. Eat up."

Carol agreed, pointing a fork with dripping runny yolk at me. "You two sound like my mama and daddy. Miri, it's good to see you."

Miri appeared to blush at that, nodding at Carol. She looked embarrassed. Why did she look embarrassed? "Thank you for the invite."

Ms. Enid turned to The Starlet. "Mel, darlin', I heard you've got a big movie coming up in the fall. Tell us about it!"

With that, the topic was dropped, for now.

We settled into comfortable conversation after that, and I made sure to shove my mouth full of food whenever Miri spoke. Miri made quiet conversation with Carol whenever I spoke.

Carol was in the middle of showing pictures of her toddler nephew smiling with a tiny row of baby teeth and jam on his lips. At first, I didn't even notice Miri had slipped away from the table.

While everyone was distracted, I checked my phone. We'd have to be at tables in a half hour. The poker room was a quick walk across the lobby, but I wanted to get going. Give myself a chance to start the day's play with a clear, methodical mind before doing battle.

I flagged down the server.

The tradition was whoever was still in the tournament paid the breakfast tab. Since Miri was nowhere around, that would be me.

Good thing, too. Hearing her suffer through a thank you for buying breakfast would be too much this early in the day.

The server greeted me with a smile. "Is there something I can do for you?"

"Yes, thank you. I was hoping to close out and pay the bill?"

She looked confused. "There was another lady. Pretty lady with the pink dress? She settled the bill already."

Ah, crap.

"My mistake."

Miri strutted back to the table, barely suppressing a smirk.

I ground my teeth, grimacing as my guts knotted.

This was another way for her to assert her dominance over me. I couldn't let her get the better of me. Not today, not ever.

"Thanks, Miri. You're such a sweetheart." I forced a smile through gritted teeth.

Ms. Enid patted my wrist in sympathy. Her voice was acid-sharp. "And always full of surprises."

Carol, though, she really looked touched. "You really didn't have to do that, kid," she said, softly.

Miri squeezed her hand. "It was my pleasure, Carol. Truly."

Was there something I was missing here?

My skin prickled with something. Interest, annoyance, whatever. Maybe I had my head up my ass, and Miri wasn't using this situation as an opportunity to one-up me?

I looked around the table. The servers made quick work of gathering plates, silverware, and napkins. The ladies started to disperse. Carol caught my look.

"She's a ball buster, but she's not all bad," Carol said. "She's more decent than I thought."

Miri? Decent? Is this the Twilight Zone? Where were the cameras?!

Carol continued, her face softened. "Look, Jax. You know I don't go around tellin' my business all willy-nilly. As such, this conversation stays between us."

I shook my head. "What conversation?"

Carol said, "I would've lost the house if it wasn't for her."

"Oh wow," I said, for lack of words. What?!

Carol smiled, shaking her head in admiration. "Don't tell anyone I said this, but Miri is good people."

Day 3 at the tables. At $300k in chips, I was holding on by my fingernails with the short stack.

I had a bar date with a Scotch neat, and my old beat up copy of my favorite poker book to give me a refresher on what I was doing wrong.

The odd thing was we had switched tables halfway through. Miri wasn't at mine, either time. It felt odd. I don't know how else to describe it, but looking over and finding someone completely uninterested in anything but the hand in front of them felt weird. Made my skin itch.

I promise I wasn't going to the bar to run into her, or anything like that. Scout's honor. But after my conversation with Carol this morning, I did have something to say to Miri.

So that's why, when I spotted her there first, I didn't hang back and wait for the next elevator down. Instead, I walked right up to her. My heart thudded faster with each step I took, but I forced myself to look her in the eye and smile.

"Hey," I said, "how'd you do today?"

Miri looked at me like I sprouted three heads. "Fine." It wasn't much of an answer, so I kept going. My mouth ran away with me before my brain even had a chance to catch up.

"It's funny," I said. "It felt like you weren't at any of my tables today."

Miri raised an eyebrow and narrowed her eyes slightly before she spoke. She didn't seem amused by my attempt at a joke.

"That's because I wasn't," she replied coldly. "So why don't you tell me what your point is?"

She wasn't going to make this easy. Fine. "I just wanted to say thanks for this morning."

"How big of you to notice," she quipped.

Me and my big mouth weren't done. Never seemed to be, not when it came to her. "And, of course, you had to ruin it. So, congratulations, I guess."

"Jax Bass saying thank you?" Miri tilted her head, her voice dripping with mockery. "Did I wake up in some alternate universe?"

"Maybe you did," I replied, trying to maintain the civility as it ticked away faster than we would descend floors. This was going to be an interesting ride. "Or maybe you could just accept the fact that I was trying to be nice." I said.

She let out a dry chuckle, eyes glinting like the business end of a knife. "Nice? Coming from you, that's as rare as a straight flush."

"I can surprise you sometimes, you know," I shot back, unwilling to let her have the last word. "Maybe you should keep that in mind for tomorrow."

Her smile turned predatory, and I could feel the familiar tension rise again between us. "Oh, I'll keep that in mind, Bass. But tell me, are you going to actually show up tomorrow? Or will I be playing against the girl who folds quicker than a lawn chair the minute anyone puts pressure on her?"

My pulse quickened with a mix of irritation and adrenaline. "Do you always have to take a dig at me? Can't you just accept a thank you graciously?"

"That's no fun, now is it?" Her smirk was infuriating and, yet, incredibly alluring. "Besides, Jax, you should know that you're moving to the deep end of the ocean now. Water you haven't swum in just yet. Everyone left is good. You're going to have to up your game."

"Oh, I've got game." I folded my arms. "Maybe you're just too busy picking off all the fish to notice."

"And if you're supposed to be so good, why haven't I seen it?" Miri countered, gesturing at my book. "Maybe you skipped a few chapters, darling?"

"Oh, fuck you, Miri." With a flourish, I held out my arm to motion her to walk into the elevator first. I expected Miri to step back and wait for the next elevator, but she stomped inside.

She wasn't pouting anymore; she was mad. Like, legit, honest to goodness upset. "No, fuck you," she said, glaring. "This is a tournament. I'm here to win this fucking tournament, and you are in my way. And yet, all I can think about is you! Do you know how frustrating that is?!"

Her words slapped the air, and I almost backed off, but my feet carried me closer to her. Something about that moment made it impossible to look her in the eye, so I focused on her parted lips instead. Her cheeks flushed red. Her chest heaved. Mine pounded a rhythm I knew all too well. What was happening?

Everything was suddenly too loud. Her breathing. My heart stuttering against my chest. That stupid fucking classical version of some yacht rock song I probably sang on the ride over here.

"Miri," I begged. "Don't." Except, I was standing so close to her I practically said the words right into her mouth.

"You feel it, too." She wasn't asking. "What are we going to do about this, Bass?"

It would be so, so easy to shut her up so she didn't say anything else that might awaken this thing between us. Preferably with my mouth. Or, sweet Lord—my tongue sucking on hers.

I clenched my fist as my brain played out white-hot flashes of what we were going to do about it. My hands grabbing at her ass. Her leg cinched tight around my waist. My body pressing hers into the mirrored panes. Hungry mouths licking, sucking, biting. Us giving some security guard a show. Damp panties straining against my wrist as I buried wet fingers inside her. Fogging up all the mirrors with our breath, our lust. I could lose myself inside her. I just knew it.

The two people reflected back at us were unrecognizable, but also the truest form of the both of us. It shot straight to my gut like a Molotov hitting the ground and exploding into hot fire. This wasn't Miri trying to win a tournament. I did this to her. We do this to each other.

We wound each other up because it was safer than touching this hot, hot stove between us. Yet, it was always us daring the other to be the first to touch it.

What if I wanted to touch that stove to see how hot it would get?

My grandma, my old lady, used to say lovin' and hatin' weren't that different. They both keep you up at night.

Is that what this is?

"I want you." Stupid, stupid words from my stupid mouth.

Miri's shook her head in annoyance. "Finally, Jax. You're as stubborn as they c—"

That damn cinnamon perfume was dizzying, made my brain foggy. That's it—I lost my fucking mind. That is the only way I could explain kissing the last word from her mouth.

Pulling her close, the electrical shocks shot straight through my fingertips. All my nerves woke up at once. This wasn't longing, but hunger. A curious, pulsing want. Even as I kissed her, part of me wanted to push her away. My fingertips begged to touch her hair. Her bare shoulders looked so soft; I needed to learn their texture. My lips needed to kiss the nape of her neck, my tongue craved the taste of the arch of her back, the inside of her thighs. As the kiss deepened, Miri tugged hard at my jacket, grounding me right back into the unthinkable. Out of my head. So urgent, like she could feel the parts of me wanting to flee. The pulsing spread an ache to the deepest part of me.

Neither of us heard anything, but the chill from the lobby broke us apart. Our kiss had an audience. I froze. Oh, no.

The Starlet turned to Ms. Enid. "You owe me. Pay up."

Carol raised her over-plucked Lucille Ball eyebrows at us. "Well, shit! I was pulling your leg when I said get a room, but I like the way y'all think!"

KING OF SPADES

MIRI

I stared down at the worn deck of cards in my hands, running my fingers over the frayed edges. Piotr's deck. The cardboard was soft and supple from years of use, the faces no longer crisp white but faded to an ivory yellow. I remembered watching Piotr's aged hands shuffling these very cards countless nights, the soft swish as he bridged and rifled them. This deck had history.

I peeled off the top card and turned it over. The King of Spades stared back at me, the once black ink now muted to charcoal. Piotr's favorite. He'd always considered it a lucky draw, though I'd scoffed and dismissed it as superstition.

My thumb brushed over the King's wrinkled face, and I was flooded with memories of Piotr. The first time he invited me to one of his legendary cash games, though I was still learning the game. The way he taught me to watch the eyes, not the hands. His patience as I fumbled through beginner's mistakes. Late nights over vodka, picking apart hands and strategies. He was kind to me when other people looked down their nose at me, and I never forgot that.

I never had a dad. Mama never said who it was. But Piotr would've been the closest thing I ever had.

Most of all, I remembered his wisdom. "Emotions have no place at the table, Mała," he'd said, his accent clipping the vowels. "Passion—passion clouds the judgment. Play the player, not the cards."

I shuffled the deck slowly, Piotr's words echoing in my mind. My thoughts drifted to Jax and the heated kiss we'd shared last night. In that moment, something between us shifted. The icy wall between rival and lover had cracked.

But what did it mean? Were her feelings genuine, or a new angle for her to use to hurt me? I couldn't deny my attraction to her, but I knew better than anyone how emotions could destroy a player.

I stared down at the faded King of Spades and made a decision. Whatever this thing with Jax was, I would deal with it later. At the table, I needed to stay focused, keep my head clear. Play the player, not the cards.

For now, Jax and I were still opponents. I planned to keep it that way.

I gathered the cards and shuffled again, focusing my mind on the tournament ahead. But, unbidden, memories of Jax crept in.

The first time we'd played in Atlantic City, the crackle of tension between us had grown with each new height in the stakes. With grudging respect, we recognized a worthy opponent. Late nights spent analyzing hands, probing each other for weaknesses.

Somehow, we turned out to be each other's biggest weakness.

Over time, our rivalry had turned into something more. Lingering looks across the table. Barbs shot in between hands. A different tension whenever we shared the felt.

I couldn't pinpoint when friendly competition had turned into attraction. But last night had brought it to the surface. I still felt the urgent press of her lips on mine, the way she'd trembled against me. It was more than lust. For an unguarded moment, her icy facade had melted.

What did it mean for us? Were we ready to be more than rivals? I didn't know if I could trust her with my heart. But I couldn't deny what I felt, this magnetic pull between us.

With a sigh, I tucked away the cards. I had a tournament to focus on. I could figure out Jax later—preferably with no cameras around. For now, I had to play the game, not the woman.

Piotr was right. Emotions were dangerous at the poker table. Whatever Jax and I shared, it would have to wait.

I took a deep breath and steadied myself. The kiss had cracked open the door between Jax and I, revealing new possibilities. But I couldn't let myself get distracted now. The tournament waited for no one.

My mind drifted back to the reactions of the crowd after our public display. The shock on their faces, the excited whispers behind raised hands from people who weren't even there. Many saw it as a juicy piece of gossip or drama, something to dissect and analyze. They didn't understand the complexity of our relationship. I don't blame them. It was sipping piping hot tea, not something they had to live.

Was it real? Or another angle Jax was playing? I hated doubting the genuineness of her feelings. But Jax was always calculating, ruthless in her pursuit of victory. I couldn't rule out the possibility the kiss was designed to throw me off balance before the tournament.

If that was her plan, it was certainly working. I was questioning everything between us. The tender moment I had believed was real. Had she been playing with me all along? Using my attraction to destabilize me as a competitor?

No. I refused to believe our connection was artificial. Some things you can't fake. The passion, the heat—it had to be real. But I also couldn't let my judgment become clouded. Not with two million on the line.

I had to approach Jax and this tournament like any other opponent and match. Focus only on the gameplay, the odds, making the right reads and calls. I could figure out the rest later. For now, I had to lock down my feelings and do what I came here to do—play my best game.

I took a deep breath and pushed aside all thoughts of Jax and our complicated relationship. I needed to get centered and mentally prepare for the tournament ahead.

Shuffling through the worn deck of cards, I thought back to my early days with Piotr. He had taught me so much about keeping emotions separate from gameplay. "Be cold as ice at the table, Maka." he would say.

I used to scoff at his advice, thinking I could balance my personal life and poker without a problem. But I've slipped up before. Like with the messy women's basketball player who liked being messy, then found out very quickly I didn't.

I couldn't let that happen again with Jax. As intoxicating as our chemistry was, I had to keep her at a distance, but especially during gameplay. Treat her like any other opponent. The bracelet and two million were mine for the taking, or mine to lose.

I took one last deep breath and steeled my nerves. No more distractions. Eyes on the prize. Time to do what I came here for.

APPLE FRITTERS AND REGRET

JAX

I didn't just wake up on the wrong side of the bed. I woke up in the wrong bed. My own.

My phone was hooked up to my charger. I drained the damn battery dry last night with hours and hours of mindless videos. Anything to erase my thoughts about the kiss. About her.

Not just thoughts, either.

My skin still tingled with the memory of soft lips, pushing out any thought of strategy. Damn near bit my own lips clean off last night as it played out in my head, over and over again. The book I brought to the bar was useless. Words I had read many, many times before stubbornly rearranged themselves not to make a lick of sense.

Much like everything else in the last day or so.

Most people, they find someone they like, their stomach twists in knots thinking of the next time they're going to see that person again. I knew we would see each other again. Across the felt, staring each other down to win the same bracelet.

Getting ahead of myself, here. Worrying about tomorrow never did anyone any favors, but I had to be ready. I had to be focused, ready to strike. There was no room for distraction. No hesitation, no matter that I knew what her kisses tasted like.

What Miri had said in the elevator stung, but she was right. I had gotten too soft, folding at even the tiniest hint of trouble. It was time to tighten up.

I got out of bed and grabbed a shower. The water stung hard and hot against my skin, helping me shut out everything but the sensation of drops hitting my back. I had to be ready for what comes next. I stepped out of the shower, dried off, and went about my morning routine of getting ready.

A quick check of my phone gave me a half hour to make it to the tables without sacrificing any blinds I already couldn't afford to lose. This morning, a quick coffee and a muffin would have to be enough to get me through the day.

If I was lucky, I wouldn't bump into her.

***

The quickest way to grab breakfast was at the little stand next to the casino floor. The glass display held all kinds of mouth-watering pastries dripping with glazes, syrups and berries. Maybe I'd treat myself sometime to a warmed up cinnamon roll with glaze oozing down the sides. This morning, a regular muffin would do the trick.

Ms. Enid had the same idea I did, except she had allowed herself the apple fritter.

I guess when you're her age, you can eat whatever the hell you want.

Ms. Enid was about to hand over her card to the cashier, but I waved her off. "Uh, actually, I've got this. Both of these."

She smiled. "If you're feeling really generous, I could use a new car, too."

I laughed, and she quickly added, "But these will do. I'm sure you need the money for the tables later today." She motioned over the table with the sugar packets, creamer, and stirrers.

My smile faded a little bit, and I nodded.

Ms. Enid stirred a pink packet into her black coffee as she spoke. Straight up, like she was. " I know you have a few minutes to tables, so I'll keep this short. I was young and hot in the tail once, a thousand years ago." She gave me a knowing look. "No matter what I tell you, you're going to do what you want, and that's how it should be. You're grown."

"I hear a but coming, Ms. Enid." I wished I could have heard a small sinkhole opening up to pull me into oblivion, too, but we can't always get what we want, right?

"But, keep your eyes open. This still is a tournament, and she is your opponent. Acknowledge your feelings, but don't let it throw you off your game." She nodded toward somewhere over my shoulder. I didn't dare follow her gaze. After yesterday, I didn't trust myself to even look at Miri across the room, but I could feel her nearby. This new heightened awareness was annoying. Yet, it rushed through me, even though I was helpless to stop it.

I got what she was saying: don't let Miri's kiss distract me from the game. "You know how competitive these things can get."

"Yes ma—"

Enid glared.

"Yes, Ms. Enid."

I turned toward the poker room, only to see Miri ahead of me, slipping inside, the door closing behind her.

She hadn't even bothered to say hello. Not even a 'we need to talk'.

Huh.

Was she doubting this, too?

Shaking my head, I turned and walked toward the back of the poker room. The final table was set up like a TV studio, with bright lights and high-end cameras capturing every action on the felt. All around me, I could feel anticipation in the air as players jostled for position. Everyone in the room was there to win—or at least have a chance at it.

I found my seat among nine other players from all walks of life: young guns eager to prove their worth; old pros looking for another shot at glory; seasoned regulars who'd been grinding for years; and a few wildcards thrown in for good measure. Then there was Miri.

The cruelest joke of all was the one seat left at the table was the one to the right of her. I'd have to sit through the day's play inhaling her scent and feeling her body heat next to mine. Wanting to kiss those bare shoulders. Remembering that uncertain look in her eyes when we kissed for the first time, and the kiss itself.

All while fighting for two million dollars, and my first poker bracelet.

Someone out there hates me.

As I settled into my chair, the energy built up around me. None of it was comforting—not with Miri sitting to my left. We hadn't spoken a word to each other since yesterday's kiss, but I could feel her presence radiating throughout the room like electricity.

Fear shot through my veins as I looked at her. She sat stiff straight and counted her chips. Eyes darted quickly around the table, then back down at her chips. Not making aimless conversation like she usually did.

I don't know which was worse, being frozen out like this, or being the target of her constant roasting.

I rolled my eyes at myself. Like some sitcom teen sulking that the person who used to nag them for attention had moved on. Maybe she had the right idea: just win.

IF YOU CAN'T SPOT THE FISH...

JAX

The glare of the overhead lights burned my eyes as I stared down at my cards. A decent starting hand, but nothing to write home about. Across from me, Dawn fidgeted in her seat, chewing on her bottom lip. The rookie was easy to read, her nerves written plainly across her face.

I kept my expression blank, giving away nothing. My focus needed to be on the game, on dragging my dwindling stack of chips back from the brink. But my gaze kept sliding to the left. To the woman seated next to me.

Miri.

Her thigh pressed against mine beneath the table, a subtle point of contact that sent sparks skittering across my skin. She toyed with a chip, flipping it deftly between her fingers, as she eyed the pot. When she glanced my way, the intensity in her chocolate eyes made my breath catch.

This was our dance, this push and pull between us. Bickering like sitcom neighbors during the day. At night, I thought about what it would feel like to lose myself in her body, over and over again.

I couldn't afford the distraction today. Not with five other women gunning for the two million bucks. But no matter how I tried to focus, my mind kept wandering, replaying the way Miri had clung to me hours before...

Damn it, I needed to keep my head in the game. Thinking about kissing your opponent had to be written down somewhere in some poker manual, double-underlined, italicized, and bolded: No good. Miri was using our connection to throw me off, I was certain of it. I couldn't let her succeed.

Squaring my shoulders, I met her gaze directly for the first time today. Her full lips curved into a hint of a smirk. My heart stuttered, but I held strong.

She wasn't going to be the first to look away. Fine.

I tore my eyes from Miri's and surveyed the other players instead. Some familiar faces had made it to the final table. Veterans like Gertrude, who I'd tangled with before. But one woman was new to me.

Eshe Landry.

I watched her toss in a hefty raise, grinning slyly as the other players folded. She was bold, aggressive. She kept thick, dyed locs long and piled off to the side in a high ponytail. In a dark button down shirt with peekaboo tattoos on her forearms, she dressed masculine like me. Landry liked to talk shit in a Creole drawl between hands at the table, but her easy gap-toothed smile let everyone know it was all in fun. From what I've seen of her, she looked like the type to bluff big and push people around, then slow play the nuts to throw you off balance. I'd have to be careful with her.

The dealer flipped the next cards—Jack of Hearts, Ten of Spades. I had pocket Tens, a strong starting hand. I tossed in a bet, testing the waters.

Martha called, her wrinkled face giving nothing away. Landry considered me for a moment before raising again, higher this time. The rest of the table folded.

It was time to make a stand. I re-raised and pushed a tall stack of chips into the pot. If Landry was bluffing, I would put a dent in her stack right away.

She didn't blink. Just calmly called my bet.

The turn revealed a King of Diamonds. I bet again, but Landry called once more. My palms grew slick. What did she have? Was it better than my trips?

When the river came up Queen of Hearts, I knew I was in trouble. Landry smirked and went all in. No bluff—she had the nuts with a hidden Ace.

I sighed and folded my Tens face down. It was a bright, blinking sign I missed being so eager to take her out early. I glanced at my dwindling stack and waited for the next hand.

Stay focused, I told myself. One hand at a time. But my eyes drifted back to Miri, seeking her out like a compass needle toward true north.

Miri caught me looking and flashed a coy smile, her eyes sparkling with mischief. I quickly glanced away, trying to focus on the cards being dealt.

But I could feel the heat of her gaze still on me, willing me to look back at her. To be distracted. To lose my edge.

I picked up my cards with slightly shaky hands. King and Eight off suit. Nothing special but playable. I called the big blind and tried not to react when Miri deliberately brushed her arm against mine, sending a jolt up my spine.

"So, Jax," she purred, "ready for me to take the rest of your chips?"

I kept my eyes fixed straight ahead. Don't look at her. Don't get sucked into her banter.

"In your dreams," I muttered.

She laughed, low and throaty. "In yours."

Heat rushed to my cheeks. I struggled to keep my composure. This was her game—throw me off, get in my head.

The flop came—Ace, Ten, Three. All off suit. I checked, wary of the Ace.

"I'll bet you that Ace is mine," Miri taunted.

Damn it. I couldn't resist a glance at her then, catching the sparkle of delight in her eyes.

"What do I get if I win?" I asked. My mind flashed hot with an image of Miri's face buried between my thighs, slick mouth taut, drawing pleasure out of me with her tongue.

Jesus, fuck. My thighs tensed involuntarily. We had gone from bickering to teasing sexual favors at the poker table. This was going to be a long ass tournament.

I took a deep breath and tried to focus on the other players, avoiding Miri's amused grin.

To my left sat Cherie, a nervous-looking woman who looked like she was in her late twenties. Her fingers fidgeted with her chips as she watched the action unfold. She had been playing tight all day, folding more hands than she played. I could tell she was intimidated by the experienced players at the table.

If she wasn't my opponent, I'd tell her scared money don't make money.

Across from me sat Gertrude, the veteran had a curly pixie cut that looked fresh pressed from the salon. Her ageless face was set in a stoic mask, giving nothing away. She looked like she had been playing poker since before I was born. I hadn't played with her much, and didn't know much about her style, but she seemed capable of mixing it up when the situation called for it.

The rest of the table was filled out by solid, if unremarkable, players. Miri and Landry were the real threats. Miri with her unconventional tactics, and Landry with her hyper-aggressive style.

The dealer burned and turned the next card—a Five that didn't change much. I checked again, leery of the Ace still looming.

"Scared of that Ace, Jax?" Miri purred. "Don't worry, I'll go easy on you."

I bit my tongue to stop a retort. She was trying to throw me off, and it was working. I couldn't let her get to me. Not now, when it mattered most.

The river was a Deuce. Useless. My King high was likely no good. I checked again, bracing myself.

"Seventy thousand," Miri fired out.

I stared at the chips in front of me, calculating odds. With her Ace she likely had me beat. But folding here could be a mistake.

The sound of chips clinking echoed through the room as I agonized over my decision. I was dimly aware of the crowd watching, waiting to see if Miri's tactics would pay off. All I could focus on was her gaze, daring me, challenging me.

I was in dangerous waters here. But I had to take a stand sometime.

"I call," I said evenly, and flipped over my useless King high.

Miri slowly turned over her own cards and my heart sank. Ace high. She had me dominated.

The crowd erupted into cheers and catcalls as Miri dragged the pot towards her growing stack. I felt my face burn, but kept my expression neutral.

One hand lost. But the tournament was far from over. Miri may have won this round, but there was still time to catch up.

The clink of chips and shuffle of cards filled the chilly air as I watched Miri from the corner of my eye. She sat to my left, spine rigid, eyes narrowed in concentration. The bright lights of the casino reflect off caramel skin, highlighting her high cheekbones.

"All in," Miri said, pushing her stack of chips forward. Murmurs rippled around the table. She's ramped up her aggressiveness now that we've made the final table, all traces of hesitation gone.

The dealer turned over the flop—two Queens and an Eight. Miri didn't flinch, even as the player to her left, Landry, raised. I folded, not willing to risk it.

Miri considered her cards, lips pursed. Her tells were subtle, but I spotted the minute tap of her index finger on the felt. She was nervous. My pulse quickened, hoping she didn't make a mistake. This was too important for both of us. I may have wanted new things from her, but the desire to stare her down at the final table was still very much present. That hadn't changed.

The turn card was a Ten. Landry stood over her cards, eyes glinting. "Let's finish this."

Her bravado surprised me. I had seen Miri make bold moves, but never reckless ones. The river came, and they turned over their cards—Miri with the third Queen, and Landry holding nothing but Ace high.

Miri took the pot with a satisfied grin. I let out a hard breath. She was still in this. We both were. And I'll be watching her every step of the way.

I reached for my glass of water, fingers accidentally brushing Miri's as she did the same. We both froze, eyes locking. Her touch was electric, even for a fleeting second.

"Sorry," I muttered, yanking my hand back quickly like I had touched a hot pan without gloves. Miri looked flustered, a faint blush rising on her cheeks.

The dealer announced play for the next hand had started. I tried to refocus, but my skin tingled where it made contact with Miri's.

She seemed affected, too, fumbling her chip stack and almost knocking it over. I had never seen her this rattled before. It gave me a strange sense of satisfaction, knowing I could throw her off her game as much as she threw off mine.

This tournament was a rollercoaster of emotions between us. Rivals, enemies even, yet undeniably drawn to each other. Every shared glance, every subtle reaction noticed only by the other—it all added up to this undercurrent neither of us can deny. Other than a quick, stolen kiss in an elevator, I didn't know where it would lead after today.

All I knew is I need to keep my head clear if I was going to beat her. Miri glanced at me again, one arched eyebrow raised in challenge. Game on.

Miri eyed her hole cards, then tossed in a raise. I expected Landry to re-raise, trying to push Miri off a hand, but she called.

Miri bet again on the flop. Landry put in a big re-raise. Miri didn't back down, re-raising herself. They were locked in some kind of weird pissing contest and I was happy to be out of the way.

The turn card came. Landry fired another bet. Miri paused, studying the board. Her brow furrowed; lips pursed. She looked uncertain.

She's bluffing. I stared at Miri, hoping she'd read my look. This wasn't trap betting not to scare off any action at the table, this was scared betting because she was holding nothing.

Miri tossed her cards away, folding. "Nice hand," she muttered.

Landry flipped over her cards—Ace high, like I thought. She bluffed Miri off a big hand. Miri looked stunned as the dealer pushed the large pot to Landry.

She muttered under her breath loud enough for the mic to pick up. "Should've stayed in. I had her beat."

Miri rubbed her temples, no doubt mentally kicking herself. She avoided eye contact with the other players.

I was shocked, too. It was so unlike Miri to make a mistake like that. She'd always been able to read her opponents flawlessly. But I probably would have made the same mistake, too, as wildly unpredictable as Landry had been all afternoon.

You play differently against someone you know than you do against someone you don't.

Landry smirked as she stacked her new chip stack. Miri's stack shrank, by a lot. She avoided my gaze, jaw clenched.

This changed everything. Miri was the fish at the table, and Landry just got her first whiff of blood. She'd be gunning for Miri, taking advantage of any weakness.

I wish I could offer some gesture of support, but we were still opponents here. Instead, I caught Miri's eye and gave her a small, encouraging smile. She returned it half-heartedly. I could tell she was still beating herself up over the hand.

If anything, Miri is tough as nails. She took a deep breath, squared her shoulders, and turned her focus back to the game and re-stacked her chips.

But I knew her confidence was shook. And I needed her to stay strong if I was going to take her down myself later.

Miri played it safe over the next few hands, keeping to modest bets and folds.

She seemed hesitant to put many chips at risk after that last misstep.

I couldn't blame her—with that one hand, she'd gone from a commanding chip lead to being perilously low on chips. A few more bad beats and she was out.

The other players started to circle around. They raised Miri more often, trying to knock her out. To her credit, she didn't take the bait, sticking to her tight strategy.

Kind of like me the first day of the tournament. Someone out there has to be laughing at this; me playing like her, and her playing like me.

I had to respect her discipline and focus. Lesser players would've tilted hard and busted out by now. Miri kept her cool under the onslaught and bided her time for the right moment to make her move.

Still, it was kind of hard watching her cling to life as the short stack. This was the first time she'd been in real danger of busting out since we made the final table.

Part of me hoped she could recover and make a comeback. It wouldn't feel right eliminating her so early. I wanted to take her on heads-up at the end, the way it was supposed to be.

PHILOSOPHY FOR WRESTLERS

MIRI

I stood alone in the quiet hallway, the din of the tournament a distant echo. My hands trembled, and I clasped them together, willing my nerves to settle. But my confidence was shaken, my usual bravado deserting me when I needed it most.

Today hadn't felt like me at all. The cards were against me, and I was playing on tilt, making mistakes so unlike my normal calculated aggression. Now my stack was smaller than I liked, and all I wanted was to prove myself by taking home that bracelet. At this rate, it was going to be me twirling a lone chip down the felt.

I sighed, closing my eyes. Against my will, thoughts of Jax flooded in. Jax, with her sly smile and sharp eyes that seemed to see right through me. No matter how much distance I tried to put between us, our connection was undeniable. Sitting right next to her at that final table set my skin ablaze, her intensity both thrilling and terrifying.

I had wanted space, had tried to shut her out. But the cards dealt us back together, and I was afraid. Afraid these tangled feelings for her, this unwanted vulnerability, was throwing me off my game when

I needed to be at my best. Feeling the same anxiety from her, seeing the rigid set of her shoulders when we locked eyes, didn't feel good at all.

I was afraid that, for once, I didn't have the upper hand. Life had thrown me a curveball in Jax, an unpredictable variable I couldn't account for. Like Landry's playing style, which had turned all my careful calculations on their head.

I rolled my neck around my shoulders, feeling the weight of it all. When this tournament was over, I'd need a nice, long massage to work out all these new knots.

The uncertainty ahead, both at the poker table and with Jax. For now, all I could do was take it one card at a time. Calm, like Piotr taught me.

Shaking my head, I refocused on the game at hand. I had to get my head back in if I wanted any chance at climbing out of this short stack.

My usual aggressive style had failed me so far today. Landry kept me constantly off balance, never falling for my bluffs or bully plays. She bullied me right back. Her unpredictability was a tangible obstacle, and I had to adapt.

I thought back to my initial read of her at the start of the tournament. Even then, she struck me as a wildcard—someone who danced to the beat of her own drum and didn't fit neatly into any of my mental boxes. I relied too much on putting players into categories, assuming I could anticipate their moves.

Landry was a force unto herself. Like life, she refused to conform to expectations. The only way forward was to take her as she came, hand by hand.

The break was almost over. I rubbed life back into my hands, steadying myself. Time to get back in the game. Back to the grind.

My armor might have a few new cracks, but I wasn't out of this yet. I had to stop trying to control every variable, and take the game as it came.

One hand at a time.

I stared at the felt, running my fingers over the familiar texture. The din of the tournament faded into white noise as I sank into my own thoughts.

Life was a lot like poker—it never stopped throwing curveballs. Mama used to watch wrestling when I was a kid. An angry red guy in his angry red kilt used to laugh while saying, "Just when you thought you had all the answers, they change the questions!" That was this tournament.

First came Landry, as unpredictable as a summer storm. I couldn't get a read on her no matter how hard I tried. She kept me dancing like a marionette, yanking on my strings.

Then there was Jax. My feelings toward her were...complicated. The simmering rivalry, the charged encounters, kisses in the elevator—it was a dangerous game we played, so close to the end of this thing. Doing the Tango, right up to the knife's edge.

I had wanted distance, time away to clear my head. But the cards refused to cooperate. Now her mere presence was a distraction, her piercing eyes seeing right through my artifice. Hot knife, meet butter.

For once, I felt vulnerable. Wide open. Adrift without a compass. Both the game and my personal life had me questioning everything.

I was used to having the upper hand, the one pulling the strings. Now the ground felt shaky beneath my feet.

The break ended. I took a shaky breath, steeling myself. Time to throw off these doubts and get back to business. I might not have all the answers anymore, but I wasn't going down without a fight. Jax and I had a date at the final table, just me and her.

Chin up, eyes forward, girl. Time to battle.

THE TURN

JAX

I found Miri at the hotel bar. Her usually sparkling eyes subdued, the day's losses made her proud shoulders slump a little, but a spark of defiance filled her gaze.

"Mind if I join you?" I sat down, not waiting for a response.

Miri looked up, a wry smile on her lips. "The more, the merrier."

The bartender pulled up and, on cue, set down a napkin.

"Shot of Don," I said. With a nod, he was off.

The silence between us was heavy but not uncomfortable. Not charged like it was the last time we were at this bar. Miri swirled her drink, the ice cubes clinking against the glass. The yellow paper umbrella and cherry that came with it lay discarded on the hotel napkin.

My guess was the fruit water was somewhere up in the fridge in her room.

Miri broke the silence. "You got your ass handed to you today, didn't you?" Her tone was light, but the words stung.

I snorted. "Not as bad as you did."

"Ha! You got jokes!" Miri sipped at the straw poking out of her glass, rolling her eyes. "Way to kick a girl when she's down, Bass."

Now, *that* was funny. "Add that to my *many* list of talents," I cracked a smile. When we met years ago in Atlantic City, I caught her staring. She told me to add being stared at to my list of talents. Ice pick cold glare, as she described it. She spent the rest of the night looking straight through me to the wall, especially after I won all her chips.

That had also been the night I met Dru.

"You remembered." Miri's smile faded a bit, eyes dropping to her drink. I reached over, covering her hand. A small comfort, but things between us had changed. Although we didn't seem to be trying to incinerate each other anymore, I guess a gentle roasting was still fair game.

I leaned in, lips meeting Miri's in a quick kiss equal parts apology and solace.

Miri actually buried her smile into her shoulder, hiding a blush. I made her blush.

"We should probably get some sleep," I said. I still wasn't used to looking at her and seeing her...so vulnerable. Soft. It wasn't lost on me that she was allowing me to see her this way. Had the kiss not happened, she probably would've told me to fuck off.

"Sleep? For tomorrow's game?" Miri asked, a smirk playing on her lips. Coy mischief hid in the way she traced her fingers up my arm.

At the table, there's always that voice that says, what if I've got a trash hand? Or, what if I've got the nut flush and the other guy is bluffing? That doubt. It was back, making my thighs twitch. Ms. Enid's words settled deep in the pit of my stomach.

Christ. I should've felt like I'm betraying someone. Ms. Enid. Dru. Hell, even *me*.

What was there to lose here? There would always be another tournament, another city, another prize. What was the harm of the two of us giving in to this, just for a night?

Miri looked back at me then and... Goddamn it. The urge to kiss her bobbed right back to the surface, like a plastic yellow duck in a tub. I had become Pat Arnold. Worse than Pat.

"Sleep for whatever comes next." I held her gaze until her eyes narrowed. Hopefully she realized the promise there.

"You know where to find me." Miri stood up from the bar, walking towards the door. She didn't wait to see if I was behind her.

Fuck it. I slammed back the shot of tequila and followed where Miri led.

The elevator doors slid open. Was this same one we kissed in? Miri and I shuffled in, leaning against opposite walls. Exhaustion seeping into ny bones, I studied the length of her elegant neck and swallowed hard.

Miri ran a hand through her curls. Tired dark circles lined her eyes. "Fucking Landry, messing with my plans." Her gaze flicked to me, amused. "No offense."

"None taken." My fingers curled into fists, nails biting into flesh. If I saw that smug smile again, I'd—

The doors slid shut. Miri sighed, some of the tension easing from her shoulders.

I leaned my head back, eyes drifting shut. The hum of the elevator soothed my frayed nerves as we ascended to the top floor. When this tournament was over, I'd crawl into my bed and sleep for days.

Miri cleared her throat. Her cinnamon scent enveloped me, bringing visions of tangled sheets and whispered promises. I opened my eyes to find her watching me, gaze soft.

"See something you like?"

"Ugh, again. Don't flatter yourself, Bass."

Our eyes met, understanding passing between us.

The elevator dinged, doors sliding open.

Miri grinned. "Your room or mine?"

Straight, no chaser. How I liked my women. "Yours. I could use a rematch."

"Say less." Miri grabbed my hand, her warmth seeping into my skin, and led me down the hall.

We stumbled out of the elevator, drunk on each other, clinging to whatever we could grab—a fistful of shirt, a handful of hair. Miri fumbled with her key card, cursing under her breath each time it didn't work.

Laughter bubbled in my chest at her frustration. "Here, let me."

I plucked the card from her fingers and carefully slid it into the lock. The light flashed green.

Miri kicked the door shut behind us and pressed me against it, lips finding mine. Heat sparked through my veins as I sank into the kiss, fingers twisting in her hair. She tasted of bourbon and longing, as addictive as any high.

"Finally."

"Impatient, are we?"

"You have no idea." Miri shoved me against the wall, mouth crashing into mine.

I groaned, arching into her touch. Goddamn. Every single damn nerve in my body was on fire for this woman. I had been too stubborn to see it earlier.

Breaking away breathless, Miri rested her forehead against mine. "Dammit. I can't stop thinking about you."

"Me, too," I whispered into her hair. "Ever since that first kiss, you're all I want."

A smile curved her lips. "Then we're even."

I traced the line of her jaw, the slope of her neck, desire simmering under my skin. "Not yet."

Miri's eyes darkened. "No?"

"I owe you a rematch. Unless you're ready to tap out already?" I raised a brow in challenge.

She damn near purred. "Mm. Gonna make you tap out first."

"I want you so fucking bad," I said. "You don't even know."

"Then take me."

Oh *shit*.

Miri crushed her mouth to mine, fingers deftly undoing the buttons of my shirt. We impatiently shoved it to the floor, damn near ripped it off. I sighed into the kiss, the warmth of her hands against my bare skin setting my blood aflame.

The rest of our clothes soon joined the pile on the floor.

I almost wanted her to keep her panties on, to see how much I could tease her with tongue and fingers until she tugged them off herself.

We tumbled onto the bed, a tangle of limbs and ragged breaths. Rough kisses. The feeling of Miri's hard nipples crushed against mine was my undoing, snapping layers of control until nothing remained but raw need.

I gave myself over to the tide, drowning in Miri's embrace.

Stilling her roaming hand, I said, "Patience." A slow, wicked smile curled up. "Gonna take my time with you."

"I'm not patient." Anticipation coiled low in my belly at Miri's heated gaze.

"You'll learn patience with me." I kissed a scorching trail down her neck, fingers dancing across her ribs. I bit back a comment about how many times I had seen her go all in on the flop. "Or maybe not. I might enjoy hearing you beg."

In the end, there would be no winners or losers tonight. Just us.

She leaned in close, lips brushing my ear and sending a jolt of sensation through me. "Come on, Jax." Miri's hands slid around to pull my bra. "Need you," she said.

My hands tangled in Miri's hair, drawing her mouth back to mine in a searing kiss. The feel of her bare skin against my own set my body aflame, all my senses narrowing to the woman in my arms.

I drank in the sight of her, caramel skin glowing in the dim light, full breasts tipped with tight dark nipples that needed to be tasted. Grazed with my teeth. Sucked. Miri gazed at me with eyes dark with desire, her lips parted on a soft sigh.

We moved together seamlessly in a rhythm as old as time. Hands roamed and caressed, learning the lines and curves of each other's bodies. I kissed a path down Miri's throat to her breasts and teased a nipple into my mouth. Miri arched under me with a gasp, fingers tightening in my hair.

The coil of desire in my belly wound tighter and tighter. Our hips rocked in a steady beat, Miri's soft cries driving me higher. I slid a hand between our bodies, finding the center of her pleasure slick and waiting.

Miri cried out when I caressed her folds. The sound sent me tumbling over the edge into this dangerous pull between us, pleasure exploding through every nerve. There was no going back now.

Miri met my gaze and her eyes glittered with want. Her mouth curved up in a smile as she slid her fingers into my mouth. The taste of her skin and need sent electricity through me. I ran my tongue along the length of each finger, savoring the feel of Miri's hands on me.

We fought for control of each other like we did at the tables. Most women I'd been with willingly gave up control. Miri was going to make me earn the pleasure of topping her.

I dragged my lips across the tender flesh of Miri's neck and let out a deep moan when her hands explored further down, slipping between my legs and finding that sweet spot that sent jolts through me. She teased me mercilessly until I gasped for breath, shuddering as pleasure radiated through every inch of me. Miri was going to coax release out of me slowly, making me enjoy every second.

The urge to fuck her fingers right then and there was uncontrollable. I wanted nothing more than to bury my head in her neck and rock on her fingers. But I needed her to surrender first.

I pressed her body down, meeting her mouth in a frenzied kiss, desire setting us both aflame. I moved my hips against hers in an ever-increasing frenzy, fingers searching for that bright spot inside her. Miri's hips moved in perfect harmony with mine and each shuddered breath brought us closer together.

She gasped into my mouth and I felt her pressure build until finally she seized up and cried out, gripping my arms until she gushed over my fingers.

The waves of pleasure crashed over me, too, leaving me helpless and shaking with the intensity of it all. I couldn't hold back any longer.

In one swift movement, I rolled us over so Miri was on top.

"Fuck," she said breathily, moving against my hips. With no shame at all, my legs opened even wider. I wanted every inch of her flesh on me, grinding against me. The motion made my clit slip against hers. Pushing her hips up, she sucked me in.

This time, I couldn't bite back a moan as my body tensed.

"D-do that again. God."

"You like that." The way her voice dropped was lethal. Iron fist, velvet glove. Her, riding my clit and telling me how good it felt. I wasn't responsible for how I slapped that fat ass.

Her shudder was a bonus.

The leftover tension from the table didn't go away. It only made us hold on for dear life while we rocked against each other. Release came in the sounds we pulled from each other, building in intensity until we both came again.

Spent, Miri collapsed on top of me. We both laid there looking at each other until I felt her body rumble with laughter. "What?"

I wanna know how it feels to kiss your smile, I almost said, which would have sounded goofy as fuck. Might as well stand me outside her window with a fucking boombox. Just utterly whipped.

I shook the thought from my head. Those post-sex hormones could make you sign away your house, car, and heart to the wrong person just so they can keep looking at you like that. The last woman who looked at me like that drained my back account, and I had been whipped enough to beg for more. Three whole years of more.

That's not what this night was about, anyway. We were supposed to knock off all this tension and go back to one-upping each other in the morning. Not lay up here tangled up, giving each other the stupid eyes.

"Hey, hey," Miri said. I closed my eyes and felt her knuckles brush my jaw. The essence of us lingered on her fingers. "Let's not make this weird."

That I could do. I opened my eyes again, meeting her gaze. "Fine. What made you lay down pocket Queens? Isn't that your favorite hand?"

Miri laughed, sweaty and flushed. "Zero to sixty."

We lay there in companionable silence for a while longer, until Miri finally shifted off of me and reached for the blankets.

"Come here," she said, patting the space next to her on the bed. With a sigh of contentment, I nestled into her side and let the promise of sleep take over.

Before we drifted off completely, Miri muttered one last thing. "That was quite a hand."

Surprised, I snorted a laugh into her neck and kissed it lightly before murmuring back, "How do I top that?! 'You're not so bad yourself?' I got nothing."

My eyes drifted shut, her steady heartbeat lulling me to sleep in her arms. Tomorrow the tournament would start again, but tonight I had everything I needed.

SUITED CONNECTORS

MIRI

J ax's breathing was slow and steady. Her chest rose and fell, hands slung across my hip. I still smelled what was left of her cologne intermingled with my perfume. Us.

I couldn't even remember the last time I woke up with someone like this. Usually, I made up somewhere to go, or they were already, thankfully, gone.

I propped myself up on my elbow and watched her sleep, deep in sex flashbacks from last night—her hands on my ass, her lips on my skin, our hips grinding against each other. The noises we made. Fuck, it had been perfect.

I allowed my fingers a walk up the arm holding me close. Best sex I've had in a long time, and of course it had to be with someone I argue with just for sport. Figures.

Laying here next to her, doubts crept in. Had it meant as much to her as it did to me?

She stirred; long eyelids fluttered open. She blinked sleepily, then smiled at me, a sweet shyness in her gaze I hadn't seen before.

It was disarming, this intimacy between us—so different from the electrifying tension that usually crackled in the air whenever we shared the same space.

Our eyes met and neither of us spoke. Hours ago, we'd been fierce in bed as we had been at the table. Now, as shy as teens sharing a desk in chem lab.

Jax broke the silence first. "Morning," she said in a husky voice, tucking a curl behind my ear. Her touch made the hair at the back of my neck stand up. Just like that, any excuses I had to flee died on my lips.

"Good morning."

She grinned. "Don't look at me like that unless you're ready for both of us to blind out this morning."

The idea of blowing off the tournament to go another round with her in bed was tempting. The stares from the others as we walked in with rumpled clothes and bed head might even be worth it.

I leaned in and kissed her. Our lips lingered, neither of us eager to pull away.

"Do we really have to get up?" Jax murmured against my mouth.

I smiled, nuzzling into the crook of her neck. "I don't know."

We held each other close beneath the sheets, stealing a few more blissful moments before reality set in. Jax's fingers traced lazy circles on my back, raising goosebumps on my skin. I breathed her in, memorizing every detail—the warmth of her body, the beat of her heart, the clean scent of her hair.

Finally, I reached for my phone on the nightstand. "I could order us some breakfast?" I suggested.

Jax propped herself up on one elbow. "Room service pancakes and mimosas? I like the way you think."

I laughed. "Only the best for the future champ."

Jax sat up.

I rolled my eyes. "Don't get it twisted. I mean me, of course."

"Aww, here you go." Her eyes sparkled, but she raised an eyebrow. "Champ? Getting a little ahead of yourself, aren't you?"

"Not even a little," I teased.

Jax blinked slow until she wasn't looking me in the eye anymore. She had to be looking at my lips. Then she looked back up.

Was she asking for permission?

Our eyes darted to each other's as if we were reading each other's minds. I pressed my lips to hers, softly at first and then with more urgency, as the fire between us ignited once again.

"How much time to do we have," Jax asked, tugging down the sheets that surrounded us.

"Enough."

Two of the final players of a poker tournament, we sat at a breakfast nook in our robes. Surely the staff of Lucky Skies had seen way, way worse, but still. If the bellhop was shocked, it never showed on his face.

"Jax," I said, playfully swirling a strawberry through the whipped cream on my plate. "What will you do when I knock you out of the tournament?" My voice was light and teasing, but there was an edge to it—a pointed reminder, despite our newfound intimacy, we were still competitors.

"Who says you'll even make it to heads-up, Miri?" Jax retorted with a smirk, popping a grape into her mouth. Her brown eyes sparkled with mischief.

I rolled my eyes, feigning exasperation, but I couldn't suppress a grin. Something undeniably exhilarating charged the atmosphere between us. We had touched the wire, feeling it crackle under our fingers, but here it still was, whipping with energy. The potential for more.

If she wanted it, I guess. Biting my lower lip, I swallowed the orange juice and the words that came with it.

As we finished breakfast, I couldn't help but glance at the clock. The hour was drawing near for us to rejoin the tournament, and with it came the inevitable doubts and questions nagging the edges of my mind. Did last night mean as much to Jax as it did to me? Was it just a fling, or something more? How would our deepening connection complicate the game?

"Hey," Jax said softly, breaking me out of my thoughts. "You okay?"

I hesitated, weighing my options. It was tempting to brush off her concern with a flip remark, but something in her gaze made me want to say something brave.

In the elevator, she said she wanted me.

Could I do the same?

Flinging casual insults across the felt was easy enough. But looking someone in the eye and telling them you wanted to see them again? Big, scary, vulnerable stuff.

"I'm just...wondering how we'll navigate our rivalry now that we've...you know." I gestured vaguely between us, unwilling to put words to the intimacy we'd shared.

"Ah," Jax murmured, understanding dawning on her face. She paused, considering her response. "I don't know. But maybe we don't need to have all the answers right now. Maybe we can just see where this takes us."

"Maybe," I conceded, feeling a mix of relief and trepidation at her words. It was both comforting and unnerving to know she was grappling with the same questions.

Jax hesitated and her gaze searched mine for a moment before she finally nodded. "I respect you enough to tell you this. You deserve the right to know."

My heart skipped a beat at the seriousness of her tone. "What is it?"

"Post-tournament, I'm not exactly sure what I want yet," she confessed, her voice heavy with something I couldn't place. "I'm still dealing with some stuff from a past relationship, and as much as I feel drawn to you, I need to take this slowly."

"Understood."

Well, there it was. My shoulders stiffened. I had stared down many a player, and yet, when I needed it most, my poker face was shit.

She reached for my hand. "Understood?" She raised an eyebrow skeptically. "That's it?"

"I'm not sure what you want me to say, Jax. Thank you for telling me?"

Jax sighed, running a hand over her locs. "Fuck. You're right, that didn't come out how I meant it. I—I just don't want to rush into anything and end up hurting you. Or getting hurt again." Her eyes were earnest. "I meant what I said in the elevator, Miri. I want you."

I ran my hand down her cheek. She grabbed it and kissed it, knuckle by knuckle. Sent shivers right through me. *Fuck.* "We want a lot of things from each other, Jax. I think right now is probably not the right time to talk about this." I looked her in the eye. "I think you should go."

She nodded. Before she let go of my palm, she gave it one last kiss.

I watched her wordlessly collect the rest of her things until she got to the door.

"Jax? When we get downstairs, be careful. You're still you," I said. "I'm still me, and I'm not going to go easy on you just because we..." I trailed off.

A ghost of a grin crossed her lips. "I'd expect nothing less." After a moment, she turned the doorknob. "Well...I guess I'll see you down there," she said finally, her voice subdued.

"Yeah. See you down there."

Jax held my gaze a heartbeat longer. I thought she might say something more, take it all back, and bridge all the distance between us. But the words never came.

The riskiest bet in poker wasn't suited connectors, it was this. I should've known better.

With a small nod, she turned and slipped out, the click of the door shutting behind her real loud in the room's silence. Silence I paid top dollar for.

I stood there, alone, surrounded by the wreckage of sheets still imprinted with the shape of our bodies. My lips tingled and her touch still sang across my skin.

As much as I wanted to cling to the memories of last night, the light of day had shifted everything between us. What this meant for the future, I couldn't say.

I drew in a sharp breath as I headed towards the bath. Time to put aside thoughts of Jax for now. The game awaited. With it, the chance to claim what I'd come for.

After one last glance at the rumpled bed, I turned away. My game face slid into place as I readied to face her again—this time as rivals.

We'd have to see where the cards fell after today. But for now, the next move was mine.

ON THE FLOP

JAX

L andry leaned back in her chair, arms crossed, smirking. Dark tinted glasses watching everything. She was up to a million in chips, double my stack. Her aggressive plays had paid off—for now.

Across from Landry sat Dawn, now the table fish. She had 450K left. Next to Dawn sat Miri. The thorn in my side since the day we met. Brightest spot at the table though. I couldn't help but look at her. Especially after our conversation this morning. Meeting my gaze, Miri averted her eyes to her stack, though it had dwindled to only 250K. She was struggling, and I knew she'd go all-in soon in a desperate bid to double up.

I had 675K left. Not great, but I could still make a comeback. If only Landry would stop raising every damn hand. Her relentless aggression was going to force me all-in if I didn't improve my chips soon.

The dealer shuffled the cards and slid them to me.

I peeked at my cards. Fives. Not the best, but definitely playable this late in the game. My pulse raced as I considered my options. I could limp in, hoping to trap Landry into raising, so I could re-raise all-in. Or I could open for a standard raise, inviting her to come along.

I tapped the felt. "Two hundred thousand."

Landry's eyes glinted. She leaned forward, pushing a stack of chips into the middle. "Raise you five hundred thousand more."

Of course she would. I swallowed hard, my mouth dry. It was now or never.

The dealer spread out the cards Two of Clubs, Five of Spades, Seven of Diamonds. Shit. I flopped trips!

The dealer looked at me expectantly. If I was getting the right odds, there was a 90% chance I had this one.

I didn't have as many chips as she did, but certainly enough to limp the table bully if she made the wrong call here. It was a risk worth taking.

"All in." I shoved the rest of my chips into the pot.

Miri gasped. Dawn's eyes widened. Landry smirked, clearly believing she had me dominated.

"Call." She flipped over her cards. "Two pair, jacks and fives."

My heart pounded as I revealed my pocket Fives. The turn was a Jack of Hearts. Two pair wasn't bad, but my fives had it beat as long as the river wasn't a Jack.

"Please, no Jacks," I murmured, rocking back and forth. My heart hammered against my locked thumbs. "No Jacks. No Jacks..."

The Two of Hearts on the turn was the final nail on this hand. I slammed my hand against the felt, relieved.

Landry's smug expression melted into shock. I had her. I was going to double up, and she knew it. She scowled, shoving away to wave over the waitress.

I smiled, already counting my new chips. The game wasn't over yet. But for now, at least, I had put the bully in her place.

I watched Landry sip at something that looked dark, fizzy, and strong.

Miri nudged me, a knowing grin on her face. "You enjoyed that way too much."

I felt a blush creep up my neck. It wasn't like Miri and I were actually together. We had history, sure. An attraction that refused to die. But even touching her turned me into some awkward teenager on a first date.

Landry hummed, turning her focus to the cards the dealer swept off the table. After a few expert shuffles, the dealer shot new cards across the felt.

My jaw clenched, anticipation prickling under my skin, and I hadn't even looked at my cards yet. Landry, she would be gunning for me now, looking ready to make a power play and win back her chips.

She wasn't going to make it at my expense this time.

I folded my small blind, not interested in playing a pot with her when she was spoiling for a fight. We had a long night ahead, and there was no need to rush.

Let Landry think she was in control. I knew better. When it came time to put her in her place again, I'd be ready.

The next hand dealt me pocket Queens. A chance to strike. I raised big, forcing out Dawn and Miri. Landry called without hesitation.

She wanted to play? Fine. We'd play.

The flop came Ten, Eight, Three; two were Hearts. A decent board for my hand, though the flush draw gave Landry outs. She checked, and I bet half the pot.

"I don't think you have anything." Her eyes narrowed, trying to read me. "You're bluffing."

I shrugged, unaffected. "Fuck around and find out."

Good sport she was, she grinned and bridged her cards together between her fingers.

She wanted me to reveal something, some little tell she could exploit. But I wouldn't give her the satisfaction. My face remained impassive as I waited for her move.

Finally, she pushed her chips into the middle. "All in."

My pulse jumped, excitement thrumming through me. This was the moment I'd been waiting for. A chance to wipe that smug look off her face once and for all.

I called, flipping over my Queens. "Two ladies."

Shock registered on her features before she could hide it. She flipped over Ace-Ten off suit—just an Ace high. No Heart draw to save her now.

"Nice try." I reached for the massive pot the dealer pushed over, dragging it toward me. The look on Landry's face almost made the hours of waiting worth it.

Landry slumped back in her chair, all her bravado gone. For a second, I thought she might cry, cuss, or both, and a pang of remorse flickered through me. She seemed like a good kid. Hell of a player. I had to make sure she knew that. Sucking out at the final table was always rough. A lot of people never came back from it.

I sighed. "There's always the next tournament."

Her lips twisted into a wry smile, as she shook my hand. "Jax, brah. It's been a pleasure."

I could see myself in Landry a bit. The first time I had approached Ms. Enid. My smile was genuine. "I don't know. You gave me a real run for my money, so I can't say the pleasure has been all mine, but you've got something special. Listen, if I catch you at the next tournament, we gotta link up."

She beamed, patting me on the shoulder. "Oh, no doubt! Look forward to it."

Landry stood to remove her mic pack, head held high despite the defeat. The crowd applauded as she gathered her things. Miri smiled and shook the younger woman's hand before she waved to the crowd and stepped off the platform.

Miri nodded at me, impressed.

I had learned from the master, after all.

ALL IN

MIRI

The clatter of chips and chatter of the galley washed over me as I strode back into the tournament room. One more night and that bracelet would be mine. But first, I had two more players to get through. One of whom was Jax.

My eyes found her at our table, cool as stainless steel. Her sunglasses cast a mirror over her face, but I could feel the weight of her gaze on me. I held it. Our chemistry still burned hot, a low heat I had to flick down to a simmer.

Three-handed, we had a bit more room to spread out at the table, and after last night, I needed a bit of space.

I took my seat, stacks of chips neatly arranged. "Ready for me to take you down?" I asked, my tone light despite the undercurrent. The audience murmured in response.

Jax was game to play along. "When I'm done with you, they'll be calling *me* Ms. Poker."

The dealer cut the deck and tossed me the button. I peeked at my cards—decent to start, but nothing amazing. Three-handed, I was here to play my best, not rely on the hand I was dealt. People over cards every time.

Jax raised big on the first hand, testing my limits. I re-raised enough to push back, letting her know I wouldn't be intimidated. No matter how big she thought her balls were at the moment, mine were bigger. The dance had begun. No matter how we felt about each other, I aimed to win.

Cards were thrown, chips clattered, and we played aggressively. There was an electric atmosphere as we battled fiercely for victory. Every hand had higher stakes, and I could feel the tension intensifying every minute. Dawn was trying her best to stay out of the fray, but her stack of chips decreased with each round.

Why was she still here?

Jax and I—now, this was the clash I'd been waiting for, and I wasn't giving in until it happened.

The white orbit, the dealer's button, brought us back around.

I was in big blind against Dawn on the button. Jax was the small blind, and she had already seen enough. Three-handed, the dealer button didn't matter anymore. You either took a stand or not. If you didn't, leave your chips to the winner and go. Try to win them back on the next round.

Dawn was clearly out of her depth at this stage of the tournament. I had a mediocre two pair, but I bet big anyway, knowing she would likely call to chase her flush draw.

As expected, Dawn agonized, but eventually she called. The turn and river bricked for her, and she sighed as she slid the rest of her chips my way. I felt a pang as I stacked them. Luck had gotten her all the way to the end, but this was the big leagues. Her luck had run out.

Three big blinds left. She could be holding junk, and she had to play like she had pocket Aces or she was done.

I snuck a glance at Jax. Her expression gave nothing away, but I could sense the tension building.

We were heading toward the final showdown, her and I.

The next few hands went by in a blur, my focus divided between the cards in front of me and Jax's unreadable expression. Her aggression had ramped up, as if she was trying to prove something to herself or maybe to me. I refused to let her intimidate me into playing recklessly, even though her sudden change in demeanor threw me off.

Was she trying to play like me?

I took a deep breath to center myself as the dealer shuffled up for the next hand.

I knew her tells, her patterns, her style as well as my own. We had studied each other, challenged each other, pushed each other to full tilt and back. This wasn't like her.

My first two cards were a Queen and a Jack. Strong starting hand. I kept my face neutral, not wanting to tip Jax off. She glanced at her cards and tossed in a standard open raise. I flattened my hand against the table and tapped my chips, debating my next move. Aggression or patience? My mind picked through the possibilities.

I knew which one she was expecting from me. We knew each other's moves so well, it was like playing against myself.

Dawn hadn't acted yet. But there was little she could do that wasn't an all-in. Might as well put her out of her misery.

My bet was higher than her remaining chip stack.

I turned to gaze at Dawn. "Pay to play, darling."

"Call," Dawn said. She ran a hand roughly through her strawberry blonde coif. The other pushed in her remaining chips.

"All in," the tournament director announced.

Jax whistled, sliding her cards out of play. "I'm good."

The dealer turned over the flop. Nine, Eight, Ten, all spades. I had flopped the Queen-high flush. I had the nuts.

Dawn stood behind the chair. I imagined that the announcers would have a big, fat zero next to her name on screen, because there was nothing left in that deck that could help her.

With Ten-Eight, her two pair was a dead hand.

The dealer had barely turned over the river when Dawn stood up to leave.

She shook my hand. "Good game."

"Good game," I offered, giving her a sympathetic nod as she stood up to leave.

Which left the two of us, Jax and I.

So many mixed feelings in this moment.

I hated the way things looked on camera, the two final opponents staring each other down as the lights went dark. Cameras moved around, panning over the felt. Zooming in on the dealer. Scrolling out over the cheering audience as spotlights danced and the lights came back on.

Yet, with the two of us looking at each other, it was every bit as dramatic as it looked, and only we understood why. It was our own little inside joke.

Our eyes met across the table. The energy between us was palpable, like the calm before a gathering storm. This was the moment I had been waiting for, for years. A chance to finally prove I was the best by defeating the one player I wanted to beat above all others. To settle the score.

May the best woman win.

SUCKER FREE SUNDAY

JAX

Heads-up poker is a very different animal from a table full of vets and fish. With more people at the table, you pick and choose if you want to see a flop or not. One on one, that Four-Seven of Spades you'd lay down looks at least worth a shot. Or, something to bluff at.

Miri leaned in, passing the chips of her short stack back and forth between slender fingers.

"You must need a Diamond," she said, looking at the flop, then slow-eyed it back at me. "Are you looking for a flush?"

I kept very, very still and looked at my hand again. Still Two-Three of Diamonds. I didn't dare tell her I need a diamond as big as the one she was wearing on her right hand. Preferably an Ace or a Five. "You tell me."

Pink nails arranged chips in stacks of orange, red and blue. I looked at the flop to keep from looking at her in the eye. I've seen her in all her glory, savored her taste, and for some reason looking her in the eyes across the felt too intimate.

Me, in the rigid set of my body, I was giving away nothing. But Miri's superpower was she could read the things people hide. The flirting was always a smoke screen; it disarmed people long enough for her to figure out what they want and what they have. *This* is why she has two championship bracelets.

If I read her just as well, Miri was going to make me sweat this one out.

She tapped her cards. "Check."

The dealer flipped over the turn card. The Six of Spades?! No help.

Miri tsk'd and sat back in her seat. "Ooh. You missed the turn, didn't you?"

This hand, it must've look crazy to the announcers. If she had nothing, I could take down the pot with a simple bet. If she's baited me, I'm already dead. Kinda wanted to see this river, though, to let me know just how dead I was. Then, kinda not.

If I had anything at all, even a low pair, I should call. All I had is a hope for a Five, with a whole lot of cards still left in the deck. Either way, I was an open book. I was the fish, and she had me wiggling on a hook.

Better to lose a hand to live to fight another day. If I went all in on hopes and dreams and lost, I'd never live it down. Instead, I tossed my cards on the felt. "Fold."

Miri took a deep breath in through her nose and batted long lashes at me. "Aww, you're no fun."

"Says the woman who's about to take my bracelet," I shot back. "Can't let you do that."

Miri shrugged and raked in the pot. "Oh, but it matches my other ones."

I glanced down at my chips. $2.5 million chips as the short stack to her $4.7 million. These blinds weren't getting any cheaper. Something needed to happen, and soon.

Usually, as the night wears on, the casual fans retreat to The Strip to drink and yell at nothing, leaving only the faithful. At one a.m., the crowd in the gallery was still live. Our dealers switched shifts an hour ago. With the rest of the ballroom dark, the glare from the studio lights made me reach for my sunglasses.

Miri's pink Manolo sandals rested at her feet, switched to slides. Hair tied up in a messy bun.

I probably looked every bit as tired as I felt. We both did.

A stack of chips piled high next to Miri's fingers told a tale. She had won some of my chips, and I had won some of them back.

I don't believe in God sometimes. That's probably why He kept giving Miri the good cards.

As the dealer shuffled the cards, I rolled my neck and cringed at the crack it made.

"Someone needs a nap," Miri said.

I laughed. "Oh, Miri. Only if you put me to bed."

Now, that got her attention. She sat up a little from resting her elbow on the table and cleared her throat. Her face blushed as pink as her shoes. Sex flashbacks from the night before assaulted me, as I felt the ghost of teeth biting into my shoulder.

The dealer slid cards across the felt as I pushed in my chips for the small blind. Still smirking, Miri put the big blind in the middle of the table.

I took a deep breath before looking at my hole cards.

King-King, Clubs and Hearts.

The glasses probably kept my eyes from bugging out a little. This was potentially a bracelet-winning hand, but only if I played it right.

I made it a point not to touch my chips. Not yet.

Across the felt, Miri looked at her hand. Her face gave away nothing, but she picked up a chip and twirled it.

Must've liked that hand. So much so she gave it a second look.

The dealer burned the top card, removing it from play. The flop read: King of Diamonds, Ace of Hearts, Two of Clubs.

Trips again! Maybe someone out there liked me, after all.

Miri was dead quiet. Shuffled her chips. Looked at me, then looked at the pot. She came back to herself after a moment.

I stopped myself from tapping the felt. Miri was too smart a player to go for that. Perhaps she'd respond to aggression instead.

I pretended to hesitate for a moment and carefully nudged my chips to the pot. "All in."

I can only imagine what the announcer team is saying. Whose highlight reel is this going to end up in? Mine or hers?

"The funny thing is, I can't figure out if you really liked that flop or not," Miri said, dryly.

"Only one way to find out."

"Finally, we agree on something," Miri said. She bit her lower lip. It was a moment before she pushed her own chips forward. Because I had more chips than she did, if she was wrong, her tournament was over. She frowned at me. "Call."

The murmur from the gallery rose.

Whatever the outcome of this match, I would always remember the look of surprise on Miri's face when she took in my pocket Kings. She rolled her eyes in disgust and stood up.

"Un-fucking-believable." She groaned. Miri turned over her cards and walked away from the table, with her hands on her hips.

I rose from my chair.

The turn was a blank, but the river brought an Ace of Spades. She was drawing dead, and she knew it.

I had a full house, Kings over Aces.

Miri mucked her hand and leaned over her chair. "Nice game, Bass." She looked me in the eye and smiled as she said it, but there was something sad about it. She looked resigned. My heart sank.

"Nice game," I said, numbly. "Miri, I—"

Everything went quickly after that. The tournament director brought out the bracelet, the confetti fell from the ceiling, loud cheers from the gallery.

A reporter appeared from behind me and shoved a microphone in my face. It was so chaotic, all I saw was a sharp angled bob and blood red lips. "Melissa Chen, Poker Babes Online. Could I get in a brief word?"

"Sure, yeah," I said. The crowd continued its celebrations. People slapped high fives and a chant broke out with some variation of my name.

Microphone shoved in my face, I babbled something to the interviewer about how it felt to win my first bracelet. I looked around the crowd of people celebrating.

Before she stepped off the platform, Miri paused and glanced over her shoulder toward me. Our eyes met across the room, and a strange sensation washed over me—an odd tangle of emotions I couldn't quite pin down, but which included a hint of warmth, admiration, and, I guess, respect.

She had earned that respect long ago, though I hadn't given it to her.

Then she gave me a curt nod and pushed through the doors, leaving behind only a cloud of disappointment in her wake.

I had been so focused on beating her it never once occurred to me I would feel such conflicting emotions when I did.

I nodded back, and turned to the reporter.

"That was an intense heads-up match," Melissa said, her eyes lighting up with excitement. "You couldn't hear, but they were going *crazy* in the booth with the back and forth! What did you think of Ms. Poker's performance? Where does she rank among your toughest opponents?"

I paused for a moment before I replied. "Miri is definitely one tough cookie, no doubt. She's incredibly fierce and strategic, and people don't give her enough credit for that. She has scary intuition with those cards and just reads people very well. Plus, she puts on an intimidating face to throw people off their game—but ultimately she's just a really great player. Definitely one of the toughest opponents I ever faced. I look forward to the rematch. Whenever that will be."

"And we can't wait for that rematch! Again, Jax, congratulations! This is Melissa Chen, for Poker Babes Online..."

As the last claps began to fade, a familiar voice cut through the noise. I moved through what was left of the crowd, shaking hands and thanking the folks who stayed up late. Someone shoved a cellphone camera in my face and asked for a quick selfie.

"Looks like you finally did it, Bass." Even over the hum of the crowd, I'd know that voice anywhere. How long had she been standing there? A chill ran over my skin.

I turned, and there she was. Dru, looking as flashy as ever. Cat eyes and bow lips pulled into a smirk. An emerald silk dress hung in loose waves around cocoa shoulders, with the white gold chain I had given her nestled between ample breasts. She was leaning against the rail, a smug grin on her face, waving white-tipped nails at me. Beside her stood a woman who could've been my mirror from a few years ago.

"Dru," I said, my voice steady. My heart fluttered, but I pushed it down. This was my moment, not hers.

"Aren't you going to introduce me, babe?" The woman next to Dru said, already taking a step forward, her hand outstretched. "I've been hearing about you all evening."

I glanced at Dru as her grin grew wider. She was enjoying this. But I wasn't the same person I was when we were together. I'd grown, changed.

"I bet you have," I said to the woman, but ignored the offered hand. I turned back to Dru, looking her in the eye. "You haven't changed a bit, have you, Dru?"

Now the woman looked confused. "Y'all know each other, for real?"

I leaned in. "One thing I can say about Dru, she certainly has a type." Dark glasses, oversized white tee, Jesus Piece as long as the dreads peeking out from a bucket hat. As much as it pained me to admit, this was probably me when I first met Dru.

Dru's mouth opened slightly, caught off guard, as her companion looked at her in question. "What's that supposed to mean?"

I nodded toward them as I turned to go. "Y'all have a good night now."

I heard Dru's new friend suck her teeth. "Stop playing with me. Who is that?"

Me? I was nobody. Not anymore.

Ms. Enid used to play with an older Polish dude, Piotr Mazur. Bless his soul. Loud dresser. His balding blond hair went silver early, and he had the best cigar laugh ever. One of his favorite sayings was "not my circus, not my monkeys." As I walked away from the crowd, I finally understood.

On Tilt

Miri

The lingering scent of lavender hit my nose as I turned off the light to the bathroom.

My muscles ached, and my head throbbed from staring at cards all day. I walked past the hall mirror and saw my tired, makeup-free face staring back.

With a sigh, I collapsed onto the plush hotel bed. The silky sheets were cool against my skin, but did nothing to soothe the turmoil in my mind. I replayed every hand, every fold, every call. Where did I go wrong? How did Jax read me so easily?

I rubbed my temples, trying to massage away the creeping self-doubt. I used to trust my poker instincts completely. But this final table against Jax had rattled my confidence. The run in with Landry the day before had exposed all my secrets, I bet. Showed her how to crack the Miri code at the table.

Maybe my feelings for her had clouded my judgment. I thought I could separate the game from my budding attraction, but the way Jax got the better of me today proved otherwise.

She expertly used my own strategy from my own playbook to win, ultimately beating my pocket kings with aces over fours. I missed her slow-playing a monster hand. Stopped thinking with my brain. Ugh.

I groaned into my pillow, angry at myself for letting her get to me. This loss was on me, not her. I had to get control of my emotions if I ever wanted to redeem myself in a rematch.

With a deep breath, I cleared my mind and focused on the soft bed enveloping me.

Couldn't do it.

I tossed and turned instead, unable to quiet my racing mind. The day's events kept replaying—the electric tension between Jax and I at the table, the admiring glances from the crowd.

The smug look on her face when she revealed the winning hand.

In the harsh light of defeat, doubts always crept in. Jax was the one who played a masterful game today. I was the one who had cracked hard under pressure.

I bit my lip, remembering how I flirted with Jax, convinced I could put her on tilt and gain the upper hand. Instead, she saw right through me.

I had worked so hard to be taken seriously in this world. Now, with one careless performance, I worried I had lost all credibility. The basement-dweller fanboys would eat this one up. I could almost see the blog posts and the breathless fanboys with their clickbait videos saying maybe I didn't deserve the respect I thought I had earned. Maybe my peers were right, and I really was little more than a bimbo who relied on looks over skill, after all. I could win ten more bracelets and still wake up to the same shit. It was the nature of being a woman in a man's game. Nothing was earned. Everything was given away, to be taken by someone who didn't deserve it as much.

These toxic thoughts swirled as I stared up at the ceiling, willing sleep to come take mercy on me.

Tomorrow, I would start fresh, rebuild my confidence, prove I was more than just a pretty face. But tonight, my brain would play back that last hand over and over again. In IMAX. With surround sound.

I replayed key moments of the tournament, analyzing my strategic errors, both off and on the felt. Losing stung, but realizing I let emotions cloud my judgment hurt more.

I convinced myself Jax's flirtation meant she cared, but this was high stakes poker—not romance. The game came second to nothing, not even love. Like. Whatever this was.

In my silly attraction to her, I lost sight of the game. The more important thing. Jax capitalized on that, though I can't call it manipulation. She saw a strategic opening and took it. Can't fault her for it. How many times had I done that myself?

My cheeks burned hot with embarrassment. I had worked hard to be respected, only to make amateur mistakes. I should have compartmentalized the attraction better.

As much as it pained me, winning was Jax's priority in the end. But maybe our connection wasn't entirely an illusion. The sparks between us felt real. You can't fake chemistry like that.

As much as I wanted to blame Jax, I had to own my part in this. I'm the one who allowed myself to get flustered and distracted by the tension between us. She capitalized on it, yes, but staying focused was my responsibility.

I had a day of flights ahead of me, and a bruised ego determined to keep me awake. I needed me to stop dwelling on the "could have beens" and focus forward on redeeming myself.

This wasn't the last tournament. Whenever we came face to face at the felt again, I'd get my lick back. Bet.

Still wide awake. On the television, some huge, bright blue gemstone twirled on a ring stand, as some saleswoman with frosted blond hair teased high to the gods tried to convince people to buy it.

She so was good, I had almost pulled out my card for a moment.

I tossed and turned most of the night, thoughts of Jax swirling through my mind. Our flirtatious banter, the smoldering looks, her lips pressed against mine in a surprise kiss at the bar. Feeling the shudder of her coming apart underneath me as she buried her face against my neck in pleasure.

Had it all been calculated? A way for her to throw me off and claim the title for herself?

The more I considered it, the more confused I became. Did she really care about me, or did she just want to win? Or was just it safer for me to think she really didn't want me?

Exhaustion finally took over in the early morning hours. My dreams were restless, full of snapped straight flushes and Jax's taunting smile as she raked in her winnings. Enid was the dealer, for some reason. Every win, my stack shrunk as Enid's hands kept slapping cards down, working faster than a blur with each deal.

I awoke late the next morning, groggy and disoriented. No chip on my shoulder, lest she take that one, too. The blackout curtains didn't even let in a sliver of light.

Good. Let me be extra dramatic as hell and sulk in this cave of darkness instead.

I ordered breakfast from the private chef, too heartsick to face the crowds downstairs. Might as well use up my amenities this one last morning, while I still could.

As I scrolled through the social media timeline, an interview with Jax popped up. Landry had reposted it with a prayer emoji, and hashtags #legends #respect, and tagged me. I clicked the video, watching Jax come to life. She had deep dimples that popped against cocoa skin when she smiled real big.

She talked up my intuition. Said I was an intimidating opponent, and one of her toughest. Huh.

The knock on my door startled me.

"Room service."

I sat stunned, breakfast forgotten that quickly. Was she being sincere? Or just trying to soften the blow of her victory?

It settled on me then. Maybe—just maybe—could I have been wrong about her?

Feasting on a slice of grapefruit, I rewatched the interview, studying Jax's face for any hint of deception. The earnest look in her eye gave me pause. Her praise seemed genuine, her compliments sincere. She spoke of our showdown with respect, even saying she was ready for the rematch.

My anger melted away, replaced by confusion. I had been so sure Jax was using me, toying with my emotions for her own strategic advantage. But now...I didn't know what to think.

Maybe I had misunderstood her intentions. Let my own insecurities blind me to this big, scary thing really happening between us.

Jax was a fierce competitor, but she wasn't cruel. If all she wanted was the win, she wouldn't be so gracious now. She had proven herself honorable in victory and defeat.

A spark of hope rekindled inside me. My feelings for Jax weren't one-sided after all. She respected me, as a player *and* as a woman.

Our rivalry wasn't over—Jax was itching for a rematch as much as I was. She said so. But perhaps it could be something more. A battle of equals, opponents who pushed each other to new heights on the felt. And in love, let the chips fall where they may.

I smirked as I watched Jax on the screen, her competitive fire clear even in an interview. My hurt and anger evaporated. She was a worthy adversary, and I couldn't wait to face her again.

This time, with a fresh set of tells.

I turned off my phone and set it aside. I had heard what she said, loud and clear, the first four times. Continuing to watch after that was just an excuse to stare at her face again.

Jax was real. No matter what happened after this, our moment of connection had happened. It was real.

I stood and stretched, working the kinks out of my back and shoulders. It had been a long tournament, and I was exhausted in body and spirit. But I felt lighter now, like a weight had been lifted.

Going to the bathroom, I caught my reflection in the mirror. For the first time in a while, I saw myself clearly. Not Ms. Poker. Just Miri.

I splashed cold water on my face, wiping away the last traces of overnight face cream. The armor wasn't needed today, and away from the felt, I had no one to perform for.

After changing into comfy pink sweats, I pulled my hair up in a simple ponytail. My fuzzy edges could probably use a good silk press. I had to laugh at how ordinary I looked. No makeup, just moisturizer.

The people downstairs wouldn't recognize me without the designer dresses and heels. I could blend right in and slip out the door in peace.

Maybe that's what I needed. To lick my wounds in peace.

I slipped on my favorite pair of high-top sneakers with the wild patterns that matched absolutely nothing and laced them up tight.

I hadn't won two million dollars, but half a million wasn't nothing to sneeze at either, as Mama would say.

I could take a long Mediterranean cruise—paid for with my tournament winnings—and not be on anyone else's clock but my own. Might treat myself to that and remind myself of who I was. Am.

I'm still that bitch, and I will never let anyone forget that.

Win or lose, I knew I'd suit up again. And I'd get my next bracelet then.

NICE TO BEAT YOU

JAX

The next morning, I woke up with one sock on, still fully dressed, and the mother of all hangovers. My head pounding, driving back to L.A. now sounded daunting. The traffic, the tailgaters, the smog. I didn't want to deal with any of it, but driving out here had been my own damn brilliant idea, and now I'd have to deal with it.

A quick check of my phone messages revealed a round of congratulations, with several insisting the next dinner and drinks were on me. Only Ms. Enid offered to fly me out to her house in wine country to celebrate winning my first bracelet. With the stipulation I brought with me the signed Ace of Hearts I had won with yesterday, of course.

Excuse me while I die of happiness.

There were, blessedly, no more messages from Dru.

The one person I wanted to talk to, though, hadn't reached out at all, and it bothered me more than I liked. What would I even say to her?

Sorry I beat you? I wasn't, not quite. I proved myself, just like I wanted. Won my bracelet.

The guys. They bust each other's balls at the table all the time. Then, they go home, drink expensive liquor together and laugh about losing a year's salary on a bad beat. No one takes it personally. Except that one obnoxious dude nobody likes.

There was no reason it couldn't be the same with me and Miri. Right? I thought the moment in the elevator had changed everything for us. Certainly, the way I felt about her had changed. I hoped she knew that.

I looked at the wall as if I could see her on the other side. Was she thinking of me as well? Maybe I should go punch that wall or something, to stop feeling so damn soft about this. Ugh.

I nearly shuffled into the shower to let the water melt away the tension in my stiff muscles, but stopped short.

Maybe I was stalling the long drive as much as possible, but I could afford the late check out now. Maybe I wanted to see Miri's face one last time, who knows. I was the Women's Invitational Poker Tournament champion, and champions take long, hot baths.

I filled the deep spa tub with hot water and a few drops of sandalwood oil. I sunk into it, letting the heat surround me like one of my grandma's hugs.

Grandma didn't hear too well these days and barely watched anything that wasn't a court show, so I'd have to fly back home to tell her in person. The thought of seeing my old lady's age-weathered face made me smile.

Before long, every muscle in my shoulders and back were completely relaxed for the first time in days. Weeks, if I was being honest, courtesy of Dru.

I thought of Miri, who had won the last few tournaments and had made it to the final table again on her own skill and grit. I was happy for myself, but felt a twinge of sadness for her, too.

She had worked so hard and deserved it as much as I did. Although she hadn't reached out to me yet, I knew her loss disappointed her—despite her usual poker face. I didn't like where we left things yesterday.

That's when, annoyingly enough, I started to feel guilty. What if she thought for a moment there could be something between us, that we could be more than rivals, and then I just...won?

Did I play with her feelings unfairly? Was there any way a relationship could work between us? I knew Miri was tough, but these last few days showed me some of the softness she pretended wasn't there. Hidden behind sharp words and aggressive plays. She let me see the woman instead of just the player, and I responded by telling her I needed space.

Wonderful.

The championship bracelet was shiny, but it was not a crystal ball. I didn't know how we'd work in the real world if we tried, or worse, what would happen if we didn't. Just pack up the cards and forget about everything between us.

I couldn't imagine looking across the felt, seeing some sarcastic comment build behind her eyes, only to be pulled back at the last moment.

That would sting more than any insult.

I sighed and closed my eyes. There were so many thoughts scrambled up in my head, and nothing seemed to make sense right now. The remnants of last night's tequila didn't help one bit.

For now, all I could do was accept my win graciously and face the consequences of it later.

The elevator took longer than normal, but that was to be expected during checkout. The wheel of my suitcase caught in the gap between the hotel floor and the elevator. I didn't look up, I pressed the button to the lobby and waited until the gilded doors closed.

"I believe you're wearing my bracelet," someone said. I looked up. The smile that spread across my face was genuine, but I would play along.

"No, ma'am. I won this fair and square."

Miri regarded me with a nod and extended her hand. "Indeed, you did."

Looked like I would finally get that handshake, after all.

"Then I'll have to win it back from you during the rematch." she said. Fresh-faced, she was even prettier. "Until next time?"

"I look forward to it," I said, shaking it. I toyed with the idea of not letting it go. Not letting *her* go. The two of us, giving the cameras another show just for the hell of it. Seeing the unasked question in my face, she raised her eyebrow as her cheeks flushed deep red. I cleared my throat, letting my eyes linger on her parted lips for a moment before meeting her gaze. "Beating you again, I mean."

This time, she laughed as she poked me in the chest. "We'll have to see about that."

I caught her hand and held it there, watching her eyes widen. We locked gazes for a moment as the elevator went down, down, down. Our lips were so close, they barely brushed. Whisper-light kisses. One breath. The soft ding of the elevator broke us from the spell.

The next tournament was in October. Might even consider putting up my own money for the chance to see her again. Maybe before then, if I played my cards right.

"See you in Madrid?" I asked, but it sounded wrong even to my ears. Still trying to keep from exposing my hole cards, I guess. After all we had put each other through, wasn't it time to stop leaving things to the luck of the draw? C'mon, Bass. Do better. "Or, I could take you out to dinner?"

Her smirk gave away nothing and everything. "Your treat."

THANK YOU!

Thank you so much for reading Bad Beat! I hope you enjoyed reading it as much as I enjoyed writing it!

If you wouldn't mind, would you be kind enough to leave a review?

Bad Beat on Goodreads.

Also, if you want to keep in touch, please feel free to subscribe to **my mailing list**. Or, use the QR code below:

*

And finally, for a sneak peak at the next book in the series, turn the page!

PREVIEW: TAP OUT

"I can't believe it," she murmured. "This sport is sooooo brutal. I don't get the appeal."

Heat flushed through me. I turned, ready to set her straight, but she continued chatting with her friend, oblivious.

"Barbaric," she said with a delicate shudder. "No technique, no artistry. Just sheer violence."

"You don't know what you're talking about." The words flew from my mouth before I could stop them.

She turned, eyes widening. "Excuse me?"

"You heard me." I faced her fully. "If you think MMA is just brutality and violence, you're wrong. Dead wrong."

"Really, girl?" She lifted her chin. "Enlighten me then."

"It's a science," I said sharply. "Strategy. Applying the right techniques at the right time. You have to understand your opponent, find their weaknesses. Use your strengths against them."

She gave me a patronizing look. "And beating each other senseless accomplishes that?"

"It's a fight," I snapped. "In a controlled environment with rules. The better fighter wins through skill and preparation."

"Whatever, girl. If you say so." She turned away dismissively.

I seethed, hands clenching into fists. How dare she belittle my life's work? MMA was an art form, a chess match of the body. She understood nothing.

I opened my mouth to tear into her again when the lights dimmed. A promo for the main event played on the big screen, tugging my attention back to the Octagon.

I huffed a sharp breath, willing the conversation to end. The last thing I needed was a debate with a cage side spectator. I needed to focus. My title defense loomed, and distractions were not an option.

I nodded to the ring girl as she approached, championship belt draped over her forearm. Its familiar weight settled across my lap, the metal plates smooth and cool against my fingers.

My name boomed through the speakers, followed by a graphic splashing across the Jumbotron. My face, big as day. Grayson "Lights Out" Dawes—Women's Featherweight Champion, it read.

The crowd erupted. I lifted my belt in the air, and thousands of voices cheered my name. This was the moment I lived for—the lights, the energy, the anticipation.

"That's you?" The woman's shocked voice cut through the noise. "You're the champion?"

I turned to her, lips curving. "Surprised?"

Tap Out is the second sports enemies-to-lovers novella in the *Competing Desires* series coming in early 2024. **Join the waitlist** to get a pre-sale link as soon as it's available.

THE END

9 781737 815419